WITHDRAWN
Sale of this material benefits the Library.

WITHDRAWN
Sale of this material benefits the Library.

"When things heat up,
don't fight. . . .
Just run."

The Trap Door

Lisa McMann

SCHOLASTIC INC.

For Casey
—L.M.

Copyright © 2013 by Scholastic Inc.

All rights reserved. Published by
Scholastic Inc., *Publishers since 1920.*
SCHOLASTIC, INFINITY RING, and associated logos
are trademarks and/or registered trademarks of Scholastic Inc.

No part of this publication may be reproduced, stored in a
retrieval system, or transmitted in any form or by any
means, electronic, mechanical, photocopying, recording,
or otherwise, without written permission of the publisher.
For information regarding permission, write to
Scholastic Inc., Attention: Permissions Department,
557 Broadway, New York, NY 10012.

Library of Congress Cataloging-in-Publication Data available

ISBN 978-0-545-48456-5
10 9 8 7 6 5 4 3 2 1 13 14 15 16 17

Cover illustration by Chris Nurse
Book design and illustrations by Keirsten Geise
Back cover photography of characters by Michael Frost © Scholastic Inc.

Library edition, February 2013
Printed in China 62

Scholastic US: 557 Broadway · New York, NY 10012
Scholastic Canada: 604 King Street West · Toronto, ON M5V 1E1
Scholastic New Zealand Limited: Private Bag 94407 · Greenmount, Manukau 2141
Scholastic UK Ltd.: Euston House · 24 Eversholt Street · London NW1 1DB

Amber Waves of . . . Corn?

"FOR THE love of Madison. Er . . . mincemeat, I mean," Sera said, looking down at her fashionable yet extremely wimpy slipper shoes, which until recently had been red. "My toes are freezing." She glanced over her shoulder to make sure Riq and Dak were there with her, too, and hopefully nobody else—after their adventures in Vikingland, when a too-enormous-to-be-genetically-possible hound named Vígi had hitched a ride, one could never be too sure.

All of their shoes were covered in mud. It was raining—no, it was *pouring,* and windy, too, and they were standing in a weather-beaten cornfield. More like a huskfield, actually. The corn had obviously been picked months ago and only the tall graying stalks remained. In one direction Sera could see a small town and a sizeable river with the tips of sailing masts bobbing along it, and in another direction a few enormous plantation houses and some smaller ones, with lots of farmland in between.

Sera put the Infinity Ring back into the satchel on

her belt. They'd just used it to warp away from Washington, DC, in 1814, where they'd fixed a Break at the White House, of all places, and hung out with the First Lady, Dolley Madison, of all people. And her slaves.

That part had been a little weird.

"Where's the SQuare?" she asked. She knew they had arrived somewhere in Maryland in the year 1850, but to learn *why* they were there, she needed to check the tablet computer given to them by the Hystorians. "And if you say it's in your pants one more time, Dak, I'm going to get mad. Just warning you." Dak was Sera's best friend, but she had her limits. Hanging around with two smelly boys was getting less and less enjoyable as the days passed, that was for sure. If only they'd had time for a bath in the White House . . . now *that* would have been a story to bring home.

Home. She closed her eyes as a Remnant—like an almost-memory of something that should have been—washed over her. She wasn't sure if it was just a coincidence that warping through time seemed to make her Remnants stronger, or if these conditions met the Theory of Nonlocality, but it certainly seemed like they were related. And since Riq's Remnants were getting worse, too—even though he wouldn't talk about them—Sera was pretty sure the two experiences had to be connected somehow. Maybe the Remnants had to get worse before they could get better.

"The SQuare? It's in my pants," Dak said, which set him off laughing and slapping his thigh.

Riq, who was a few years older, rolled his eyes. "Knock it off. And be quiet. We don't know if anybody's around yet." He sighed. "I'm getting a little tired of babysitting you two. Geez."

"Did you say 'cheese'?" Dak roared with laughter again. He turned to Sera. "Did he just say 'cheese'?"

It had been a long, exhausting few days.

Sera was used to Dak's obnoxious jokes, but Riq's comment about babysitting was just unfair. Especially after she and Riq had bonded in medieval France, when Dak had been missing in action. *She* hadn't been the immature one. *She* hadn't gotten captured by Vikings or lost the SQuare or eaten the king of France's cheese or . . . or anything like that. She turned her head away, folded her arms, and hugged herself against the cold and rain as the wind whipped her sopping dress around her padded, puffy legs. She looked like a rejected yard-sale rag doll, tossed from a car window into a mud puddle.

Riq scowled. "Sorry," he mumbled. "I'm just . . . I'm tired. We all are. Come on, let's get out of this blasted hurricane and figure out what we're here to do."

Sera pushed past him, but not very hard since he'd said he was sorry, and then intentionally bumped into Dak extra hard for being so annoying. She tried to stomp down the row but one of her slippers sucked right off her foot and disappeared into the mud. "Jiminy nutcracker," she muttered. She shook her head at the spot where the useless slipper had been and kept walking, one foot bare, cold mud squelching between her toes.

She'd have taken her white elbow-length gloves off, too, if they weren't the only things keeping her from losing her fingers to frostbite.

When they reached the end of the rows of corn, Sera saw an old shed and made a beeline for it. Head down and wishing she'd at least left the White House with a parasol, she barreled forward with one goal in mind: finding shelter inside the shed.

Except for the howling wind, it was quiet. There seemed to be no one around at all. Just a shed with a door banging open, and a lantern swinging wildly on a post outside.

Sera stumbled inside, her feet numb. Dak and Riq followed her. As Sera's eyes adjusted, she saw Dak was already squinting at the SQuare.

"Well?" she prompted. "What's the Break?"

"Not sure yet. We have to solve another puzzle," Dak said. "Pictures this time." He handed the SQuare to Riq.

As Riq studied the images, Sera peered around his shoulder to get a look.

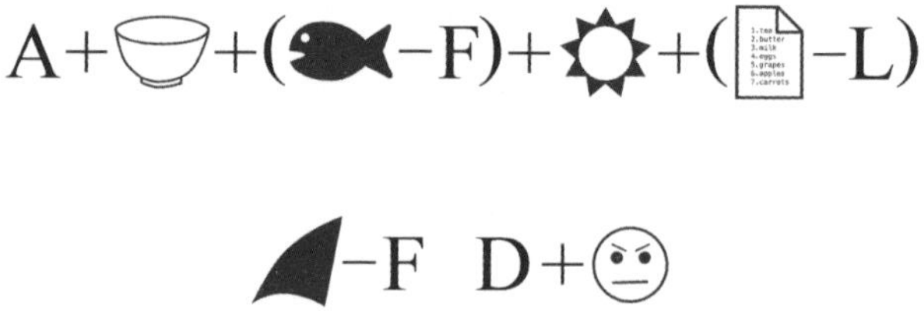

A+ +(−F)+ +(−L)

−F D+

Sera looked at the first image and began talking it through to herself. "A bowl . . . fish . . . something about sunshine food?" Her teeth chattered.

Riq flashed her a look of mild annoyance. "Do you have to do that right next to my ear? My auto-translator is going crazy trying to decipher your tooth language."

Sera clamped her teeth together and stepped back. "Sorry."

The older boy's features softened. "It's all right." He held the SQuare so that both Sera and Dak could see. "Come on. We're all on the same team. Time travelers together."

"Some of us are better team players than others," Dak grumbled.

Sera sighed and looked away, tapping her foot. She didn't want to hear any more snide comments from either of the boys. She glanced around the shed, her eyes straining in the dim light. She wondered if there was anyplace to sit down without getting completely filthy.

It was a small shed. Even in the dark, she could make out the whole space. Which is why she was surprised to suddenly see movement.

Sera froze for a second, and then took a step back so she could ease the door open, letting in a bit more light. "Quiet!" she whispered. "Did you guys see that?" She pointed to the back corner of the little shed, where the floor was moving. It was a trap door, and it was opening. "We're not alone."

Some Friend

THE FLOOR moved up a few inches, and then a few inches more. "Run!" Dak whispered. He quickly took his own advice, and it didn't take Sera or Riq any time at all to follow him out the door. They ran wildly for a minute or two, Sera hobbling through the sticks and mud on one bare foot, until they were a good distance away and hidden in a copse of evergreens.

"Why are we running?" Riq asked Dak between breaths.

"Dude, the floor moved. There was something down there!"

"Yeah, well, all we had to do was stand on it if we didn't want the person to come out."

"How do you know it was a person?" Dak asked.

"Right," Sera said. "It could have been a monster." She smirked.

"Hey, you never know. The way our luck has gone, it could have been Sasquatch," Riq said.

Dak shook his head and sighed, annoyed. "You obviously know nothing about Sasquatch. He wasn't sighted anywhere around here in 1850. Strictly northwest in the early years—he didn't even have a name back then."

"Anywaaay," Sera prompted. "This is serious—what if they heard us? Riq, you totally said we were time travelers!"

Riq opened his mouth as if to protest, but then he closed it again. "I did?" he asked weakly.

"Riq!" Dak said. "You blew it."

"Oh, please. I did not," Riq scoffed. He glanced over his shoulder nervously. "But if either of you has an idea of where to go next, I'm all ears."

Dak began muttering. "Eighteen-fifty. Maryland. A bowl something ist." He scratched his head, and then mumbled, "There was a lantern by that shed. . . ."

After a second, he looked up. A sopping brown oak leaf flew through the wind and stuck to his cheek. "Duh," he said. "Abolitionist. Come on, before we get struck by lightning." He started walking, pulling the leaf from his cheek. Riq followed him.

Sera hesitated. "Guys," she called. "I don't understand. Where are we going? We didn't solve the whole clue." She ducked as a branch came flying through the wind at her.

"Because the answer is obvious. We're supposed to join the abolitionists," Dak said. "Seems likely that our Hystorian would be against slavery, right? So we need to find one to figure out how to help them." He was getting cranky, slogging through the wet underbrush.

Sera followed along behind the boys, limping. "So where do we find an abolitionist in a hurricane?" she asked.

Dak frowned. "Technically, with a temperature this low, it's not a—"

"Well, der," Sera said, "I *know* that. It's a nor'easter, but I didn't feel like explaining—"

Riq looked up to the sky as if pleading for help, shook his head, and started trudging toward the nearest house.

Sera and Dak looked at each other and then turned to follow Riq.

"We look out of place, don't forget," Sera said, catching up to the older boy. "People might get suspicious."

He looked down at his outfit. "I'm quite aware. But we can't do anything in the way of Cataclysm prevention if we have to amputate your foot."

"Aw," Sera said. "You care about my foot." She smiled.

Riq's face was stern. "I care about the Hystorian quest."

That was enough to silence everyone for the remainder of the walk.

The first house they came to was dark. The curtains were drawn, and there was nothing in the windows or on the porch. Dak shook his head. "This one doesn't seem right." They continued to the next one, which also didn't look right to Dak.

"What are you looking for?" Riq asked.

"I'll let you know when I find it," Dak said.

Sera just bent her head into the wind and trudged after them.

Several minutes later, they approached the third house, the wind and rain slapping their faces raw.

Noticing a lit lantern in the window, Dak cautiously climbed the first porch step. "This might be it. They used lanterns as a signal." He glanced out over the cornfield, identified the shed in the distance, and wondered if the field and that shed belonged to this homeowner. If so, the trap door made a bit more sense.

Riq stopped short of the steps and frowned. *Not that there's anything unusual about Riq frowning,* thought Dak.

Sera looked at the older boy. "Do you think it's safe?" she asked.

But Riq didn't respond. Instead he groaned, pitched forward, grabbed the porch railing, and closed his eyes.

Sera reached out and held his arm. It took Dak a moment to figure out what was happening—Riq was having a Remnant.

"Is it a bad one?" Sera whispered.

There was no time to answer.

The door opened a crack, and then a bit more, and a woman in a black, warm-looking woolen dress and a bonnet on her head peered out. "Come in," she said, and then she hesitated, taking in their strange appearances. But after a moment she smiled and repeated herself, more urgently this time. "*Ooh,* interesting. Come in, come in." She waved them toward her as if to hurry them, and they didn't hesitate.

Inside, a fire crackled in the fireplace. Riq, Sera, and Dak stood in the entryway, shivering and dripping all over the floor, but the woman didn't seem to mind. She handed them each a towel so they could dry off.

"Well now," she said, looking at Sera. "Your clothes are mighty unusual."

Sera looked her in the eye. "We were at a party at the, um . . ."

"Plantation up the road," Dak continued. "It was a post-Revolutionary theme. On the way home, one of our horses, uh"—he glanced downward and saw Sera's bare foot—"lost a shoe, and we've walked quite a long way in the storm, looking for a place to stay the night."

Sera looked like she wanted to kick Dak.

Riq said nothing.

The woman smiled broadly. "There's no need to invent stories here. I'm Hester Beeson and I'm a Friend. I imagine you were looking for me." She looked at Dak and Sera when she spoke, but tilted her head toward Riq.

Dak lifted his shoulders just slightly in a shrug, and then nodded his head once.

"Right," Dak said. "Wow, so you're a . . ." He hesitated on purpose.

"Oh yes, I'm on your side," she said with a grin. "It's a joy to be of service to you." Dak's face lit up. Hystorian? *Bingo!*

Mrs. Beeson wasted no time. "Well, come along, then. We've got a safe room here—you just never know who might be about on a night like this. . . ." She led them through the house.

Dak flashed Riq a puzzled look, but Riq stared straight ahead, stone-faced.

"Can I," she said, turning back toward them with her hands outstretched, "take anything for you? Put it in the safe?"

Sera raised an eyebrow. "N-no, thank you. We prefer to hold on to everything."

"All right, then." The woman didn't seem to notice Riq's odd expression, but Dak did. And he didn't know quite what to make of it.

The woman pulled aside a plain wooden chair and a rug to reveal a square door in the floor. She turned the inset lock and pulled it open, and then stood aside and pointed proudly at the opening. "Like magic," she said with a grin. "You two and your slave will be comfortable down here."

Dak and Sera stared at each other, jaws dropped. Then Dak looked at Riq, who was bristling.

"Mrs. Beeson," Sera began, her cheeks blazing, "Riq is *not* our—"

A swift kick to her shin shut her up just in time.

"I'm glad you made it safely." Mrs. Beeson began to hum as the three climbed down a ladder into a small, cool cellar, lit by lanterns. "You'll find dry clothes to change into, and some water and soap for those cuts on your foot, miss. I'll bring some food down in a bit."

"Okay . . . thank you," Sera said, but her voice was unsure. She shot questioning glances at Dak and Riq, and they returned them. Sera leaned toward them and whispered, "She's a weird one. Do you really think she's the local Hystorian?"

Dak nodded. But something sure seemed off.

"Excuse me," he called up the ladder. "You know who Aristotle is, right?"

"No, dear," Mrs. Beeson answered. "I've never met anyone by that name."

A moment later the door overhead closed.

And then the lock clicked.

They heard the chair scraping the floor above to cover it.

The three incredibly smart, self-proclaimed geniuses had just willingly gotten themselves locked in a drafty cellar. All three turned to one another as Dak said, "Wait. What just happened?"

Quakers

"SHE MIGHT be an abolitonist, but she's no Hystorian," Riq said. His stomach fell.

"But . . . but she said she was on our side," Dak said. "Why else would she say that?"

Sera groaned. "She thinks Riq's a slave and we came here to hide him." She plopped to the floor and sat in a miserable heap. She sneezed, wiped her nose on her glove, and looked at Dak. "Why'd you kick me? I'm not going to let anybody think Riq is our slave. That's just ludicrous, and I won't do it."

"I didn't kick you," Dak said.

Riq leaned against the wall. "I did," he said. He dug the heels of his hands into his eye sockets and rubbed. He felt weary and defeated. And mad. Really mad.

"Why?"

"Because . . . well, because it's 1850, and it's complicated. I don't even know why. But I do know we can't stay locked up in here." He set his jaw. *"I'm* not staying here, anyway." He took the SQuare from Dak, who seemed happy to be rid of the device. It shook in Riq's hands as he jabbed at the buttons. He took a deep breath and let it out slowly. "Calm down," he whispered so quietly that neither of the two heard him. The SQuare powered up, casting an eerie glow in the dimly lit cellar.

"Where precisely are we, again?" Dak asked. "What city?"

"Cambridge, Maryland. December 1850." He waited a beat, and then added, "That's in the United States. They speak your one language here."

"Very funny. Well, I guess we don't need you, then."

"Fine." Riq handed the SQuare back to Dak. "Good luck."

Dak's mouth fell open. "Okay, well, try and go, then." He pointed to the ceiling. "There's the door."

"Come on, you guys." Sera let her head rest against the wall. "Riq, don't let him bait you," she pleaded.

Riq felt the heat rise in his face, which was actually sort of helpful since it was not much warmer in the cellar than it was outside.

Dak's look of surprise stayed on his face as he turned to Sera. "What, *you* think I'm a pest now, too?"

Sera glared. "Are you saying you aren't?"

"Just stop. Everybody stop it," Riq said. "Okay? I'm sorry. Sera's right. Bickering isn't going to get us anywhere."

"Who's Bickering? I thought her name was Beeson," Dak said, almost with a snort. But then he stopped. "I mean, I'm sorry, too, Ser, ol' buddy."

Sera wiped the remaining drips from her face with her sodden gloves, and then she stripped them off. "Fine. Just . . . turn around," she said. "Now. I can't stand these sopping-wet oversized doll clothes any longer."

The boys whipped around to face the wall as Sera scuffled about, changing into a set of dry clothes. She muttered as she dressed: "Just please tell me we're not in another stinking war." She flapped her arms in the air. "Sorry this is taking me so long—I'm trying to air-dry."

Dak guffawed. "Of course it's not a war. Eighteen-fifty in the United States? Well, I guess technically there was the Mariposa Indian War with California in the fall of 1850, but everybody knows California was barely a state yet, and those gold diggers just jumped right into things and took over the Yosemite Valley. And that's happening clear across the country!" He paused. "Oh, you're thinking of the Civil War, I bet. Nope, not until next decade. But, hey"—he turned to Riq—"you said that we're in Maryland, right?"

"About eighty-five times," Riq said.

Dak furrowed his brow. "Well, things are definitely heating up here between the North and the South. There was a short time when slaves were escaping to the North, many of them traveling right through Maryland, but"—he put on a snooty professorial air—"history tells us that the plantation owners put the *squash* on that, if you get what I mean."

Riq gave him a blank stare.

"The squash," he said. "Capital *S*, capital *Q*. *SQ*uash.

Get it? The SQ. Many history buffs believe the proslavery movement was not just made up of random people with a similar belief, but that there were highly organized groups working behind the scenes. Groups who had other, much greater goals in mind—like what Brint said about that guy named Lincoln who got sabotaged from being president. Highly organized groups with a secret agenda? That sounds like SQ to me. These 'unnamed groups' *SQ*uashed what were supposed to be safe houses for runaway slaves, then captured the runaways to sell them at auction, along with everybody who helped them. *Cha-ching!* How many times can you sell a slave?" He was really winding up now. "Furthermore, *some* people think," he said, clearly meaning himself, "that the Civil War wouldn't have lasted fifteen years if the slaves had been able to communicate with the Northern abolitionists and the abolitionists had gotten as organized as the proslavery groups were." Dak looked sidelong at Riq. "You linguists know what that word *abolitionist* means, I suppose."

Riq gave Dak a cool stare. "Signs point to yes." Inwardly, Riq pictured himself wringing Dak's neck. But he held back for the sake of peace.

"Okay, I'm done," Sera said. "Your turn." She wore a simple brown full-length dress with a matching kerchief at her neck and a broad-brimmed bonnet over her dark hair. Around her shoulders she'd wrapped a shawl that was a shade or two lighter than the dress, and she had found some thick socks and sturdy boots. "This is more like it," she said. "Though I could really go for wearing pants again."

Riq was glad to be in an era where pants were an option for men, at least. The dress-like tunic he'd worn in medieval Paris had taken some getting used to. Here, he was able to wear a white long-sleeve shirt and dark brown waistcoat, matching trousers, and black shoes. And a hat, too. Once he had finished dressing, he glanced at Sera in the dim light. She had her eyes closed and her forehead pressed against the wall, giving the boys privacy to change. She was still shivering in the drafty cellar despite finally being dry. Riq pulled his long jacket off and placed it over her shoulders, and then he sat down and picked up the SQuare.

She opened her eyes and turned to look at him. "Thanks," she said. She sat down on the floor. "Are you sure you don't need it?"

"I'm fine," he said gruffly. "My manliness is more than enough to keep me warm." He meant it as a joke, but like so many of his jokes, it sounded a bit mean once he'd said it.

Dak snorted and sat down. His suit was similar to Riq's, but it was too big on him, and it made him look puffy. But Riq was focused on the SQuare, studying the clue that they hadn't taken the time to solve all the way due to the storm. The answer came together in his head. He looked up, triumphant. And then his eyes grew wide.

"Abolitionist . . . in danger?" he said. "Oh, no." Had the SQuash on the safe houses already happened? Was their abolitionist upstairs for real?

Dak cleared his throat loudly, startling Riq from his thoughts. "Well, guys," Dak announced, "I figured out why I don't like this place."

"Why's that?" Riq asked. Not that it should be much of a mystery. Wasn't the fact that he'd been mistaken for a slave enough?

"That woman is not a Friend."

"Of course not," Sera said. "We just met."

"I mean Friend with a capital *F*. Of the Religious Society of Friends."

"The what?"

"He means a Quaker, a member of a religious order known for being antislavery," Riq said. "She called herself a Friend when she opened the door, remember? That's what she meant." He turned to Dak, alarmed as his own thoughts began lining up with the younger boy's. "Why don't you think she's a Quaker?"

Whenever Dak felt he had something of historical value to add to a conversation, which was often, he grew geekily philosophical for his scant eleven years of life. "Let me start by saying," he said, "I do think this is a Quaker home—you can tell by the way it's decorated. But she's not a Quaker. She doesn't talk right—most Quakers used the terms *thee* and *thou* up until the mid-twentieth century. She's wearing a black dress, and throughout history, Quakers hardly ever wore black because it could be seen as either funeral garb or as fashionable. They were all about modesty. And she probably wouldn't introduce herself as a Friend to people she wasn't sure were Quakers, too. Plus, she was awfully proud to see us, and that just doesn't seem . . . Quakerish."

"Why would she pretend to be a Quaker if she wasn't one?" Riq asked, fearing the worst. "Are you sure you're not just stereotyping her?" He didn't add, "Like she did with me?"

Sera frowned at the SQuare. "There's only one reason I can think of why she'd lie," she said. "And that's because she wanted to trap us here. You're right, Riq. She's not a Hystorian. She's not even an abolitionist." She glanced up at the trap door, and then buried her face in her hands. "She's SQ."

Stop. No, Really. STOP.

"GREAT," RIQ groaned. But he knew Sera was probably right. "Dak, what did you say about the SQ earlier? That they took over the safe houses? When did that happen?"

"Um, it was, uh, eighteen-Sasquach," he mumbled, wiping his hand over his mouth as he spoke.

"What?"

Dak nodded and tapped his chin like a professor, and then coughed, "Eighteen-abibble."

"Dak!" Sera said. "Come on."

Dak's face grew a brilliant crimson. "Welp, you see, the thing is, guys, is that, you know, really *any* of the Breaks we've already fixed could have changed the timing of things in 1850. Right? I mean, think about it. What if what we did with Dolley Madison changed things for now? Or with the Amancio brothers and Christopher Columbus? We can't be sure." He shook his head solemnly. "We just can't."

"Oh, Dak," Sera said with a sigh. She patted his knee, and then spoke, almost with a tone of wonder. "You don't actually know the answer, do you? Poor thing."

Dak frowned. He didn't look at her.

"That's okay," she went on. "It happens. Remember when I got a ninety-nine point seven five percent on my college prep chemistry exam last year? That was . . ." Her eyes clouded over and she shook her head. "That was . . . heartbreaking." She patted his knee again. "I understand what you're going through."

Dak's face crumbled. "I have it somewhere. I know I do. In a book back home. Sometimes I guess I just need a book. It's a lot of pressure, sometimes, all those dates," he mumbled. He stared at the floor. "I thought it happened later than 1850 for sure, though, or I would have said something sooner."

"Well," Riq said in what he hoped was a reasonably kind voice, "at least we know what the Break is."

"We do?" Sera asked.

"It seems pretty clear to me," Riq replied. "We need to stop the SQ from taking over the safe houses and restore the . . . whatever it is they called this effort before it failed."

Dak didn't move his downturned head, but Riq heard him mutter, "It was called the Underground Railroad. But the term never really caught on."

Riq smiled and said, "Actually, I'm a lot more interested in this Break right now than I was twenty minutes ago." But then he clenched his fists, because out of nowhere, a Remnant wave came over him again, so hard and cold and vast that it felt like his whole existence was being sucked out through a throbbing hole in his chest. He grabbed at his vest and groaned.

He opened his eyes to find both Sera and Dak staring at him with deep concern. "I'm fine," he whispered. And then he offered a shaky smile. "Let's figure out where we're supposed to be, if it's not locked in the cellar of a fake abolitionist. Shall we?"

He was glad to have the SQuare as a distraction, and he gave his full attention to it once again. He pressed the FIND A HYSTORIAN link. After a moment, the screen changed. His eyes took it in, and then he looked up. "It's some sort of word puzzle." He smiled, feeling a bit better already. "Right up my alley."

"So, it's the word *doofus* in sixteen languages?" Dak joked.

"Dak . . . ," Sera said. Her eyes were closed again. She couldn't stop shivering.

"Sorry."

Sera opened one eye and looked at Riq. "Try to ignore him. He gets like this when he's tired. He'll chill out once we get some sleep."

Dak shot Sera a look that first said, "What do you know?" and then, reluctantly, "Well, you're probably right." But with Sera's eyes closed again, Dak's looks were lost on her. He turned instead to Riq. "So, what have we got, Dr. Linguist?"

Riq moved over to sit between Sera and Dak. He put his arm around Sera's shoulders as she nodded off, feeling her shivering and knowing desperately that they needed to keep her healthy, and pointed the SQuare to face Dak. "It looks like an old-fashioned telegram," he said. He read the words aloud:

> Seek the fire not for your lantern candle oil or wood STOP Friends are friends after time STOP Tomorrows a mostly fair day STOP Visit and enjoy post breakfast STOP Office worries will wait STOP And then you can follow festivities including the eating and drinking STOP
> Sincerely
> Gourdon

"Say what?" Dak said. He studied it. "What is this, Ben Franklin's list of failed sayings that didn't make it into the Almanac? 'Friends are friends after time.' Really? I think that's the name of a pop song." Dak laughed. "'Office worries will wait'? What is this silly schtuff?"

Riq was quiet, studying the SQuare in his lap. His lips moved, and on his free hand his fingers tapped one by one against his thumb as he read the words and counted simultaneously. "I'm not sure yet," he said after a moment. "It's coded."

Dak nattered on and on about algorithms and spy code ciphers used in various wars until he had fairly worn himself out. When he had been quiet for a few minutes, Riq looked over at him. Dak was asleep now, too.

Riq smiled to himself. He was glad they were able to sleep. With all the various time changes, he really wasn't sure how many days in real time had gone by since he'd had a true full night of sleep. Somebody was always wanting to fight him, or . . . or he wanted to fight himself. His Remnants were like an inner war. And he had a feeling that this was the Break where it was all going to come to a head. It was this Break that had the potential to change his life forever—and maybe not for the better.

The Family Tree

WHEN RIQ was a little kid and his parents had to work on things with the other Hystorians, they'd drop him off at his grandmother Phoebe's house. He stayed there so often it felt like his second home, and he loved her dearly—he still did. She would quiz him on his languages, and they'd do all sorts of puzzles and word problems together. She'd talk about the traveling she had done when she was younger, all over the world, but she said she always loved coming home best of all. Her family meant everything to her.

Riq had decided then that his family meant everything to him, too. He liked the way it sounded, especially when his parents were gone . . . which was often. He thought about it when he and his grandmother would snuggle on the couch watching old Japanese and Russian movies without subtitles, and she would ask him to translate the bits she didn't understand. He liked that she needed him, and he was never embarrassed to say that he needed her, too.

Before bed, Grandma Phoebe would bring out the scrapbooks—pictures of every place she'd ever been, photos and sketches of the family dating back to the mid-1700s, which was as far back as their line could be traced—before that, they'd come from somewhere in Africa, chained up in the bowels of a ship and brought across the ocean to be slaves in America. That story always made Riq feel awful inside.

But his ancestors were brave and strong, Grandma Phoebe told him, and he was very proud to be in a family like that. Some of them were Hystorians, she said, pointing them out in the scrapbook. It was so cool to look at the pictures and imagine their lives. Riq would study the family tree and pretend to know which of the great-great-grandparents would be the cool ones who would travel the world, and which would be the embarrassing, peppermint-smelling kind who sat around the house wearing snugglies and drinking tea.

He said it out loud to his grandma one night, and she smiled. "I'm afraid you didn't have any great-greats who sat around much, my dear. We have all worked hard for centuries. See this man? He's your great-great-great-great-great-great-grandfather Jacob. He fought with the Continental Army in the Revolutionary War. And this woman here"—she pointed to a different page—"is your great-great-great-great-great-great-aunt Minty, who escaped from slavery but disappeared shortly before the Civil War. And Minty's niece, Kissy

Bowley—who was *my* great-great-grandmother—was captured as a runaway slave. Her husband, John, who was free, had tried to buy her, and her aunt Minty tried to help, but they both failed, and Kissy got captured and bought by someone else. John was captured, too, and sold back into slavery again."

"Even though he had been free? That's not fair!"

Riq's grandmother nodded. "Even though he had been free." She frowned as she finished the story, even though she'd told it a million times. "Kissy never saw John again. Years later she remarried and had another child, my great-grandfather."

"Wow," Riq had said every time he heard the story. He'd imagine the backbreaking work on a plantation, sixteen or eighteen hours a day. The mean masters with their whips, though Grandma Phoebe said a few owners had been decent. The spirituals and the songs and the families, often torn apart.

Late into the wee hours of the morning, well after his grandmother had kissed him good night, Riq hid under his covers with a flashlight and studied the pictures, memorized his ancestors' fancy names, and repeated the stories to himself. He loved learning about his family's past. He loved history. It was in his blood, but it was also in his heart. And he wanted so badly to help fix everything so all the hard work and pain and suffering of his ancestors wasn't for nothing.

∞

Now, as Riq studied the clue with the overwhelming sense that this Break would decide something major for him, he thought about his ancestors and wondered whose life had been changed because of the SQ during this time period. And what would happen to Riq if they fixed this Break? What would happen to his parents? To Grandma Phoebe? How could he risk messing with history without knowing what the consequences would be?

Maybe the only way Riq could be sure that his family history remained intact was to sabotage the mission—this one, at least.

He glanced at the Infinity Ring's satchel hanging from Sera's belt. He looked from one sleeping eleven-year-old to the other. Could he figure out how to program the Ring without either of them waking up?

But what would that solve? They'd just be furious at him for causing another unnecessary ripple, and they'd come back here anyway—they couldn't go on to the next Break until this one was done. The SQuare was the only thing that held the information to get them to the next place. And it didn't seem to want to give them anything about future Breaks until they'd fixed the Break they were in.

Maybe if he told Dak and Sera what he suspected about his Remnants, and about this Break in particular, they'd understand.

He laughed bitterly as he thought that through. "No way," he said. The last thing he needed was two little kids pitying him, or worse, sacrificing the mission to save him. He couldn't bear to have that hanging over him for the rest of his life.

He studied the words again. They began to swim in front of him. He was tired, too. Just as he was about to nod off, a few words still in focus seemed to pop out at him. He sat up and looked at them once more, then began mouthing the words and counting on his fingers again. "That's it!" he whispered.

When he heard the chair scrape above the trap door, Riq shoved the SQuare into its pouch and slipped it inside Dak's Quaker coat to hide it. Then he crept to the ladder, peering up.

The lock turned and the trap door opened.

Riq looked around wildly and hissed, "Sera!" He kicked Dak's foot. "Dak!"

They both nearly roused but fell asleep again as Mrs. Beeson's face appeared above Riq. Her half glasses rested on the tip of her nose and threatened to give in to the pull of gravity. "I brought you some bread. Climb up here and get it, boy."

Riq pressed his lips together at the slur and set his jaw, determined not to lash out. They were hungry, it was 1850, and apparently Hester Beeson was used to bossing African-Americans around. He got that. With clenched teeth, he climbed the rungs, thinking briefly about fighting her and escaping, but he doubted he'd get very far with his skin color, and he couldn't leave the others, anyway. But if he could just detain her, say, in a closet or something, he'd have time to wake up Sera and Dak, and they could all get away.

He made that his plan. He climbed a few more rungs so that his upper body was out of the cellar, ready to spring up and surprise the woman.

He reached up with both hands to take the bread. With one hand he grabbed it and with the other he clasped Mrs. Beeson's wrist and rushed up the rest of the way, tossing the bread down into the cellar. Mrs. Beeson shrieked and hit him on the top of the head with her free hand, and then Riq felt four more hands on him, grabbing him under the arms and by the shirt collar—she was not alone. "Help!" he cried. He let his body go limp to throw his attackers off balance, but they were too strong. They held him fast, yanking his arms behind his back and throwing him forward to the floor.

"There, now!" their shouts rang out. "Got you another one, eh, Mary? You're going to make a fine piece of money in the morning for this one."

Riq twisted his head around. *Mary?* The lady had said her name was Hester Beeson, and she was the only woman here. Had anything she'd said to them been true?

Riq saw the triumphant smile on her face and knew that she had been telling the truth about one thing. She'd been happy to see them. They'd walked right into her trap.

Two burly men hauled him to his feet and a third tied his wrists together in front of him. He fought off his panic, remembering the clue. "Sera! Dak!" he yelled as loud as he could. "Every third! Every third! Every third!"

He yelled it over and over until one man clamped a hand over his mouth. Riq bit down on the fleshy palm, hard, and when the hand pulled away, Riq had one last chance to scream, "Dak, Sera, *listen to me*! Every third WORD!" But then the bitten man reared back with his fist and punched Riq in the nose. All he saw after that were stars.

Bread Wound to the Face

IT WAS a blow to the face that woke Sera from a dead sleep, followed by the sounds of shouting men and pounding footsteps overhead. It took her a minute to remember where she was, and even longer to process that the thing that had hit her in the jaw was a loaf of bread, which now lay at her side. One of the shouting voices seemed familiar but nothing was computing properly in her brain.

Dak sat up, too. "What the—" He looked around. "Where's Riq?"

Tears swam in Sera's eyes—the unavoidable, just-got-hit-in-the-face kind of tears. "I heard him yelling. Did he escape without us?" She struggled to her feet, gingerly moving her jaw from side to side to see if the crusty loaf had done any serious damage. "He said he wasn't staying here, but I didn't think he'd ditch us."

"Did he take off?" Dak said. He got to his feet. "What a jerk! Why would he do that? I'm so telling Brint and Mari."

They could hear heavy boots pounding the floor above them and muffled noises. There was a flurry of activity and one last shout from Riq. "Dak, Sera, *listen to me*! Every third WORD!" The front door slammed.

It didn't sound like an escape; it sounded like an abduction. Sera and Dak scrabbled over to the ladder. Sera jumped up first and climbed as fast as she could. She reached for the opening.

Just then the trap door slammed down on Sera's fingers and she yanked them away, squealing in pain as the lock clicked. Furious, Sera pounded her fist on the wooden door above her, and she and Dak shouted. "Hey, you big bully! Open up! What are you doing? Let us out of here! What have you done to our friend?"

The only sound they heard in response was that of the rug and the chair being dragged over the trap door, followed by dainty footsteps walking away. "Ugh!" Sera slammed her hand into the ceiling one last time, furious and disgusted. Now her hand hurt, too, and her fingertips pulsed with pain. She looked up at the backside of the lock. From this side, the lock mechanism had a partial, unfinished cover over it. Sera tried to maneuver her pinkie into the narrow space so that she could push the lock open, but her pinkie was too thick and it wouldn't bend the right way. Sera glanced around the sparse cellar, having little hope for anything that could help them out of this jam.

Dak jumped down off the lower rung to the floor of the cellar, and Sera climbed down the ladder.

"Do you still have the lock pick we got from King Louis?" Dak asked.

"Wrong type of lock," Sera said. "That technology's developed a lot since 1792."

"So what do we do?"

"First thing first," Sera said gravely. She gave Dak the hairy eyeball and put her hands on his shoulders. "I'm going to ask you this question very seriously, so don't mess it up. Ready?"

"Yeah, I guess," Dak said, squirming a little.

"Okay, here goes." She moistened her lips and said, "Do. You. Have. The SQuare? Because I don't."

Dak's eyes widened. The look of fear on his face told Sera he wasn't goofing around. "Riq had it. . . ." His voice trailed off as he whipped his head around to look about the room.

"Oh, please, not again," muttered Sera. She went to the pile of wet clothing and started tossing it around the room, searching.

"Careful," Dak said, swooping in to grab a bottle of soda that Sera had thrown aside. "That's one of the first carbonated beverages ever made. It's an irreplaceable souvenir."

Sera pawed her way through the supply shelves, barely pausing to throw him a dirty look. "Did you steal that from the President's House?"

"I saved it!" Dak insisted. "Don't you remember the invasion?"

"Dak, focus! Did you check your pockets?" Sera said,

her voice pitching higher as they ran out of places to look. She went over to him and started giving him a pat down, and she wasn't gentle.

"Easy!" Dak cried.

"Hey!" Sera exclaimed when she smacked him in the chest and hit something solid. "What's this in your jacket?" She stepped back so he could find out for himself.

Dak pulled back the lapel of his jacket and found the inside pocket. "Wow," he said, looking inside it. "You could fit a whole can of SQueez Cheez in here." He reached in and pulled out the familiar leather pouch.

Sera smiled weakly in relief. "Whew," she said. "You big jerk! You scared me. How could you forget that you put it there?"

"I didn't put it there. Riq must have. Before they—" Dak bit his lip. "Yeah. That was pretty smart of him."

Sera squinched her eyes shut. It made her sore jaw hurt a little. "And he threw us the bread so we could eat something."

Dak nodded. "I guess he's not so bad."

Sera looked at her friend, the guy who had been her bestie since before she could remember, and smiled. "Like I've been telling you. He's not bad at all. He's a really decent guy. Now," she said, taking a deep, determined breath, "how are we going to find him?"

The Clue

"I DON'T know if you caught this," Dak said, feeling kind of terrible about Riq getting captured and dragged away while they slept, "but Riq was yelling something besides *help*."

"'Every third word,'" Sera said. "Yeah, I heard it. What does it mean?"

"I'm guessing he figured out the clue—it was a word puzzle." Dak pulled the SQuare out of the pouch, reentered the password ("Password") because it had timed out, and then the clue appeared again. "See, it's a telegram. STOP means to end the sentence."

"Why wouldn't they just use a period?"

"The word *stop* is understood around the world. Plus, when telegrams were sent, each punctuation mark cost the same price as a full word, but it was a lot easier to misplace a dot than a whole word, so people ix-nayed the unctuation-pay." He looked up with a grin. "Hey! I guess I know two languages after all. I can't wait to tell Riq when we find him."

He glanced at Sera and said in a more serious voice, "Because we *will* find him." He showed the telegram to Sera.

Seek the fire not for your lantern candle oil or wood STOP Friends are friends after time STOP Tomorrows a mostly fair day STOP Visit and enjoy post breakfast STOP Office worries will wait STOP And then you can follow festivities including the eating and drinking STOP
Sincerely
Gourdon

Sera read it a few times. "It would make more sense with punctuation."

"That's not the point. It's a code. What it actually says isn't really what it's trying to say."

"Yeah, I get it, Sherlock." Sera squinted at the words. "Okay, so, every third word—is that with or without the STOPs?"

Dak shrugged.

"Figuring it's with, then this says: Fire your oil stop friends stop mostly stop enjoy stop will and can . . ." She shook her head. "This is stupid."

"So take the stops out."

"Fire your oil friends after—wait, so do I skip the word *stop* only if it's the word I land on?"

"No idea. Historian here, not a know-it-all linguist."

Sera glared at Dak.

"Yeah . . . I said that without thinking, didn't I," Dak said. "I'll keep the linguist jokes to myself for now. Sorry."

"There's always a first time. Every day, with you." She struggled with the telegram for a while.

Dak took a hunk of bread and started eating. "Could really use some cheese." He handed the loaf to Sera and she ripped a chunk off, too, nibbling at it as she worked the clue.

"Ohh!" she said after a while, her mouth full. "We have to start with the first word and then do every third after that. He didn't say that."

"Shame on him for not explaining it better while being tackled and captured."

She chewed and swallowed. "How does this sound?" She read it once to herself, and then she read it out loud, guessing where the punctuation went. "Seek not lantern or Friends. After tomorrow's fair, visit post office!" Sera looked up excitedly, and then turned back to finish it. "Wait, then follow the drinking Gourdon."

Dak smirked. "'Seek not lantern or Friends.' Ahh-hahaha. Now you tell us."

"We should have figured out the clue first before coming here." Sera frowned. "It's my fault."

Dak put his hand on Sera's shoulder. "Girl-dude, it's fine. Under the circumstances, we would have drowned or frozen to death before we figured it out."

Sera went back over the words once more, memorizing them. "'After tomorrow's fair.' So we need to find the fair tomorrow."

"Then we'll go to the post office, stand around for a while, and follow some drunk guy named Gourdon."

"I guess."

"That should be interesting. I hope he doesn't ralph his guts out," Dak said.

"I hope he does. Did you know you can find out a lot about the human digestive system by studying—"

"Uhm, I kind of can't believe this, but you just grossed me out."

"Anyway, we'll get to that part of the clue eventually, but let's not get ahead of ourselves. If we don't get out of here, we'll never find the fair. Or Riq, for that matter."

"Well," Dak said, "nobody said fixing history would be easy. I guess this means we go to Plan B."

8

Captured

RIQ HAD broken his nose once before, in elementary school when he took a dodgeball to the face at close range from some crazy dude named Matt who was actually aiming for a girl. And now it was definitely broken again. He knew for sure because he could literally see the skin of his nose puffing up in front of and around his eyes. And then, of course, there was all the blood. And the pain. As the three men had dragged him out the front door and into the storm, tossing him in the back of a wagon and chaining him there, all he could do was try to ignore the pain and keep his nose protected.

But, even injured, he was a Hystorian. And he was a good one. So he also kept track of where the wagon was taking him in case he had a chance to escape. He tried loosening the rope around his wrists and tugging at the chain that held him in the wagon, but they were both stuck tight.

After an hour's ride in the dark, they came to a stop.

The men got off the wagon seat and went into a house, leaving Riq alone. He yanked and tugged at the chain, bracing his feet against the side of the wagon and pulling with all his might, but it wouldn't budge. At least the activity helped keep him warm—once again he was soaked through from rain. He wished for the coat he'd left behind with Sera.

Ten minutes later, the men came out.

Riq could sit up just far enough to see over the side. The men were leading a woman and a young boy to the wagon. They came along quietly enough, but Riq heard the cries of a baby as they approached. With surprise, he realized the woman held an infant in her arms.

At his mother's urging, the boy crawled up into the wagon, and she followed. Riq reached out his bound hands as best he could to help the little guy keep his balance in the gusty wind, as the woman climbed aboard with the baby. She held her head high and set her lips as the men chained one of her wrists to the wagon on the side opposite Riq. She did her best to shield her baby from the weather.

Riq looked at the boy, who appeared to be about five or six and was scowling into the pelting rain. "If you lie down here against the side, you'll stay dry," Riq said. "The wind blows the rain sideways and this will protect you. See? It's cozy."

The boy looked at his mother, who nodded. He scooted to Riq's side but stayed as far away from him as possible.

When the wagon lurched and moved again, the wheels bounced on the uneven, rain-soaked ground, which sent piercing pain through Riq's skull. He leaned forward. "Ma'am," Riq said, "forgive me for asking, and I apologize for my appearance, but do you know where they're taking us?"

The woman gave Riq a long look, sizing him up. "Are you a freedman?"

Riq hesitated. He knew the term, and while technically it wasn't accurate, he said, "Yes."

"So they got you with the new law?"

"Um," Riq said, "which one would that be?"

The woman pursed her lips. "You've never heard of the Bloodhound Law?"

Riq shook his head. "No, ma'am. I don't know of it."

"It passed a few months back. Used to be, the North was a safe haven for former slaves. But now free blacks can be picked up off the street in any state in the nation and sold back south. No trial. Nothing. So everybody's hunting."

Riq tried not to gape. "That's . . . barbaric."

"It's far from justice, but it's the law," the woman said. "And it gets worse. Anyone accused of helping a runaway slave is in violation of the law and has to face all sorts of trouble. It's gotten so a person can't know who to trust."

"Were . . . were you just captured?" Riq asked.

"No. Ms. Brodess has decided to sell us. We're all being auctioned." She gave him a hard look.

"*We*—meaning you three?"

She shook her head, and her words were heavy. "*We*. Meaning we in this wagon. Tomorrow. Once they get you, they don't waste time."

Riq's lips parted in shock, then clamped shut in fury. He swallowed hard, the anger burning and turning to dry ashes in his throat as a flood of hopelessness washed through him. He closed his eyelids and slumped against the side of the wagon, rain pelting like tiny stones to the back of his head. A hot tear slipped from the corner of his eye before he could stop it.

Plan B

"SO, WHAT exactly is Plan B?" Sera asked. She'd wandered over to the supply shelves and was picking through them, examining each item curiously.

"I don't know yet."

Sera smiled as she spotted a burlap bag with the words *Saltville, Virginia* stamped on it. She shoved her bonnet off her head so it hung down her back, and scratched her scalp. Then she picked up the bag. She opened it and looked inside. "Aha," she said softly to herself, and then she turned toward Dak. "Well, *I* know."

"You do?" Dak asked. "That's awesome! What is it?"

"It's time for a little chemical experiment."

Dak's eyes grew wide. He stepped back. "No way. Not like the time with the—"

"No, no, no," Sera said, impatient. "Geez, Dak will you let it go? That was third grade."

"Still, I've barely just grown my eyebrows back, thank you very much."

Sera waved off his fears. "Your eyebrows are safe. But

I am going to need a sacrifice from you."

Dak's eyes grew wider still. "Like what, like a-a—*human* sacrifice?"

"Oh, stop it. All I need is that fancy bottle of French soda that you got from the President's House."

Dak gasped and sputtered. "Blasphemy! That's even *worse*! Do you *know* how many of these still exist in our time?"

"Actually, I don't care. Because do you wanna know what?"

"What?"

"Chicken butt," they both said automatically.

"Okay, seriously, though," Sera continued. "If we don't get out of this cellar, guess how many people you'd be able to show that fancy French confectionery's bottle of soda to?"

"Well, there's Mrs. Beeson."

"In our time, you dork."

Dak scowled. "Nobody."

"Right. Nobody. But if you save the world with me, and we go back to our time as heroes, and we get really high-paying jobs and make zillions of dollars because we're so amazing, then you can *buy* a bottle just like it."

Dak nearly twisted in half with his overdramatic gesturing. "But that's the *pooooint, Seraaa*! The last authentic bottles dating back to the eighteenth century got destroyed in an earthquake! There aren't any left to buy anywhere in the whole entire universe."

"Dak."

"Whaaat?" he whined.

"Calm down."

"Right, okay," Dak said miserably. "Wait. Why should I? This is very upsetting."

"Because when we fix the Breaks and things go back to the way they were supposed to be, those earthquakes won't have happened in the first place."

Dak opened his mouth, and then closed it again. He giggled. "Oh, yeah." He giggled some more, and then he stopped. "Are you sure?"

"Positive," Sera lied. "Now, hand it over. And then we're going to rest for a little bit. We want that phony abolitionist to be sound asleep when we bust out of here."

∞

They left the lamps glowing, knowing they'd need them later, and tried to sleep. But their minds were whirring. Just before Dak dozed off, he muttered, "What we really need is a secret word that we can use to tell each other to be careful and stuff."

Sera rolled over and propped herself up on her elbow. "How about *eighteen-abibble*?"

Dak snorted. "Perfect."

A Long Night

RIQ FOUND himself out of the rain eventually, at least. He and the woman—Kessiah, she said her name was—and her two children were finally taken off the wagon and brought to the slave quarters of a plantation. They had traveled quite a long way to pick up the family, but then Riq noticed they'd turned around and ended up in the little town area not far from the cornfield where he and the other time travelers had first arrived. He recognized the ships in the harbor. It gave him hope that if he could get away, he'd be able to find Sera and Dak.

But he remained shackled, locked up in a small room with Kessiah and her children, and no matter how hard he tugged on the chain, it wouldn't come loose.

When they had arrived, a black woman wearing an apron had come to clean up Riq's wounds and give him a fresh shirt, both of which he appreciated immensely.

"Thank you for the clean shirt," he said. "I must have looked frightening."

The woman flashed Riq a startled look, and then

turned her eyes to the floor. She looked as though she wanted to say something in response yet didn't dare. She looked scared. Riq decided not to push it.

Later Kessiah told him that the woman hadn't been acting out of kindness. "You have to look good for the auction to get more bids, so they clean you up," she explained. "If you're covered in blood, nobody wants to buy you. They think you're a troublemaker."

"Maybe I plan to be."

Kessiah gave him a small smile. "'Fraid that attitude won't last too long."

Riq frowned. "What do you mean?"

"They'll beat the trouble out of you in time. They always do."

Riq sank back against the wall that he was chained to and shook his head. "You know," he said, "I really can't believe this is happening."

Kessiah shook her head, too. "I still can't, and I've never been free," she said softly.

While her children slept, Kessiah stared out the window into the darkness. She seemed agitated. Nervous.

Riq wasn't all too comfortable either, but despite his anxiety and the howling wind, he couldn't keep his eyes open any longer. He slept.

∞

When he woke up, the storm had passed and the sun was just coming up. Kessiah was asleep, and her son had snuggled up next to Riq. Riq looked at the sleeping boy, and the lump rose in his throat again. He thought about the stories his grandmother had told him, and the songs she'd played and sung for him when he was the little boy's age. The stories had been meaningful back then even though he hadn't understood the depth of them. But now he was sitting smack dab in his ancestors' shoes, shackled like a criminal even though he'd done nothing wrong, and he was about to stand on the auction block to be sold to the highest bidder like he was a horse at a trade show.

It was all so strange, but the surreal aspect from the dead of night had become very real with the dawning light. What if Sera and Dak couldn't escape? What if they did escape but didn't find him? What if he were sold to someone who took him far away? What if *he* couldn't escape either? Would he be stuck here forever to live his life out like this?

The child who sat with him probably knew nothing different for his life. Riq wondered if the little boy would ever be free.

The boy woke when the woman with the apron came into the room. She handed Riq a warm bowl of food and a cup of water. She did the same for the little boy, and then returned with more for Kessiah, setting it by her head so she could eat it when she woke up.

"Thank you," Riq said. There was corn bread and some sort of fish in the bowl. He balanced it on his knee and ate gratefully. The little boy ate the food like he hadn't eaten in a long time.

"You want some more?" Riq asked. He held the rest of his corn bread out to the boy.

"Yessir," the boy said, and took it.

"James," Kessiah said. Her eyes were open now, but she hadn't moved. "What do you say to Riq?"

"Thank you," James said.

Riq smiled. "It's all right."

Kessiah regarded him. "That was kind of you," she said.

A few women began singing outside—slaves who were hard at work on the plantation. Riq could hear them through the cracks in the doors and windows. Kessiah turned swiftly and strained to see and hear. They sang a song as they worked:

There's singing here,
There's singing there.
I believe down in my soul
There's singing everywhere.

Run, mourner, run!
Lo! says the bible,
Run, mourner, run
Lo! is the way . . .

When the song's words became clear, Kessiah sucked in a breath. She closed her eyes for a moment, and then she turned back, a look of peace on her face. "All's not lost after all," she said softly.

Riq furrowed his brow. "What do you mean?" he whispered.

"It's a song my . . . someone arranged to be sung as a signal." She looked at James and then back to Riq. "I don't dare explain right now." She nodded her head toward the boy, and then looked away. "He can't tell what he doesn't know," she said softly. When the song outside repeated, she hummed along, and when they reached the second verse, she sang out in a gorgeous voice, one line only. *Run, mourner, run.*

Riq felt something welling up inside him. He didn't quite understand all that was happening, or what meaning she was trying to get across exactly, but Grandma Phoebe had told him about the power of the spirituals, religious songs spread by slaves in the South. And for the first time since his capture, he felt hope.

They heard men's voices. "Don't fight, now," Kessiah whispered. "Do as I do."

Seconds later, the three men from the night before burst into the room, unshackled Riq and Kessiah from the rings on the wall, and hooked them together instead. Kessiah picked up the baby, and Riq grabbed James's hand as the men led them to the door and outside to the street. They walked half a mile to town as the voices of the slaves they were leaving behind grew faint. When they reached the steps of a courthouse, the men stopped and told Riq and Kessiah where to stand. And there, posted on the wall of the courthouse in front of Riq, was a flyer that made him gasp.

TO BE SOLD

BY PUBLIC AUCTION

On Monday, December 9th, 1850

In Front of the COURTHOUSE

The Four Following

KISSY, about 25, an excellent Laborer
with children:
JAMES ALFRED, about 6
ARAMINTA, an infant; and
RICK, about 16, inexperienced, suitable for
Labor or Household
The woman belonging to Eliza Ann Brodess
and the man belonging to Mary Lockett

Busting Out

SERA STOOD on the ladder, a handful of rock salt from the burlap bag in one hand and the open bottle of French soda in the other. She had changed back into her 1814 puffy bloomers and dress, with the slip tied over her hair.

"Can I at least have a taste first?" Dak asked.

"Sure, but hurry," Sera said. "And keep the noise down. We don't want to wake her up."

"Got it, chief. I'll be as far away from your mad science as possible. Trust me." He took a sip and rolled it around his mouth like he'd seen his parents do with wine. And then he made a face. "Yuck." He handed it back to her.

"Just quit goofing off and be ready."

"How is this supposed to break the door down, anyway? Is this like the soda-and-candy-reaction thing?"

"That's exactly what it is, only with rock salt—what's important are the tiny holes in the salt to create the pressure and explosion. And it won't be able to blast the door open. It's just going to unlock it."

"So, no fire involved?"

"No fire. That would be dangerous in an enclosed, windowless room." Sera gave him a patronizing smile. "Although, if only you'd had a can of SQueez Cheez . . . now that plus the oil lamp could have been a really awesome explosion."

"Stop disrespecting my favorite foods already," Dak said. He rolled his eyes and went back to the corner of the cellar. "Okay, I'm ready—I've got all our stuff in my coat, including your Quaker clothes. I freaking love this coat, by the way. So many pockets."

"Good—keep my clothes dry if you can." She swallowed hard. "We're going to experience extreme stickiness, but it can't be helped."

Dak zipped his lips and hovered against the wall. He put his Quaker hat on to protect himself further.

Sera glanced back at him, and then held her hand above the bottle. "Stay back—in case I fall."

Dak nodded. Sera figured he wasn't planning to catch her.

"Three, two . . ." Sera whispered. She wrapped one leg around the ladder to keep herself from losing balance, and she aimed the bottle toward the little hole that housed the spinning lock mechanism. "One."

She shoved the rock salt into the neck of the bottle as quickly as she could, and pointed. The liquid shot out at great force just inches from the hole, but Sera couldn't see a thing as frothy soda bubbles rained down all over her face. All she could do was squint and hope the pressure of the liquid was forceful enough to push the rotating lock a quarter turn.

It rained for ten seconds before the foam slowed. "Here," Sera said, "I saved you the bottle."

Dak ran to grab it and then retreated once again. Sera peered up at the lock. The entire ceiling above her dripped with soda. Gingerly, she pushed on the trap door.

It moved.

She did a silent happy dance on the ladder, and then scurried down. Dak turned to face the wall as Sera whipped off her 1814 clothes, wiped her face with them, and then grabbed her Quaker clothes from Dak, who had pulled them from his coat and tossed them over his shoulder to her. She got into them at full speed, and though she was still a bit sticky, it wasn't too bad. And there wouldn't be any bees around in December, she hoped. That had been her main concern about being covered in sugar.

"Remember," she said in a soft voice, "there's the little rug and the chair above the door, but with any luck you'll be able to get an arm out before the chair tips. If it doesn't move easily we're going to have to really whale on it to knock it over, and run for our lives." She patted the satchel beneath her shawl. "I've got the Ring."

Dak tapped his coat. "I've got the SQuare."

"Amazing," they both whispered together, and Sera added, "Now let's go find our friend and follow our clues."

Dak gently pushed up on the trap door. It kept going

and going, nearly to a forty-five-degree angle before it hit the chair seat. Dak pushed himself up to the next rung, his head going partway through the opening, and he looked all around. Then he dropped back below once again. "I think we can slide out without moving the chair at all," he whispered.

Sera's eyes widened. She nodded and gave him the thumbs-up.

Dak returned the gesture, and he climbed and slid up through the opening. One of his pockets nearly got caught on a nail, but Sera quickly unhooked it before it tore. In a moment, he was splayed out in the hallway. He scooted out of the way as Sera followed suit, and, being a bit smaller, had no trouble at all getting out despite the extra bulk of the dress and Riq's jacket.

But as she pulled her feet out of the opening, her bootlace snagged on the same nail that had given Dak trouble. She jerked her foot and it came loose, sending the trap door slamming down.

Sera gasped. She looked at Dak. He grabbed her arm and yanked her to her feet, and they careened down the hallway just as they heard someone coming from the next room. "Who's there?" Mrs. Beeson called out. Sharp footsteps grew louder at an alarming rate.

"Run!" Sera cried.

"Running!" Dak said.

Sera reached the front door, whipped it open, and flew outside with Dak right behind. Mrs. Beeson, or whoever she was, ran out onto the porch and into the yard after them, but she was no match for the two.

"Thanks for the bread!" Dak called out over his shoulder.

Sera poked her elbow into Dak's ribs. "Come on," she said. "Over here." They sprinted around the cornfield toward the shed they'd seen the night before. The door was closed now and the lantern was gone, perhaps blown away by the gale. She peeked in just to make sure Riq wasn't hiding inside. It was empty.

"At least the storm passed," Sera said. "Now, if you were Riq, where would you be?"

Dak looked all around. "If I were mistaken as a runaway slave and captured," he mused, "I guess I'd be either on a plantation working, or . . ."

"Or what?"

Dak looked at Sera. "Or killed."

Sera shuddered, and then she set her jaw in anger. "I don't get it. How could anybody treat another human being like that?" she cried.

Dak didn't have an answer to that one.

12

The Fair

DAK AND Sera checked the cornfield first, agreeing that if Riq had managed to escape, he might have gone there—it was sort of an unspoken rule of travel that the place you arrived was a good place to use as a meeting spot in case somebody got lost. But Riq wasn't there.

They headed toward town. "We can ask around, maybe," suggested Dak. "See if anybody's seen him."

Sera nodded. "We'll go door-to-door if we have to."

As they approached the town, things grew a bit livelier. People walked the streets, coming in and out of buildings and taverns, laughing and chatting. There was almost a spirit of adventure in the air. Dak muttered out of the side of his mouth, "Do you think this is the fair?"

Sera shrugged. "Maybe. Look, there must be a street performer over there or something. There's a crowd gathering. Act like we belong here. We should be careful in case that horrible woman shows up." She pulled her bonnet back on her head and tucked her hair back.

They drew close to the gathering and tried to peer over the shoulders of the townspeople, but there were a lot of bonnets and hats in the way, so they moved around the edge of the crowd, trying to see what was happening.

"Excuse me," Dak said, tapping a shoulder of a dark-skinned man in front of him.

The man stepped aside.

"No, sorry, I mean I have a question," Dak said. "What's going on here?"

The man glanced at Dak. "It's an auction."

"Cool. What kinds of stuff? Any unopened bottles of French soda from, say, the eighteenth century? Ish?"

Sera jabbed Dak.

The man gave Dak a harder look. He tilted his head and narrowed his eyes. "No, not that I know of. It's a slave auction." He pulled an old pocket watch with a scratched face from his waistcoat pocket, then replaced it and looked around. "Do thee read?"

"Yes," Dak said.

"Thou will find signs posted with details. It seems there is one more slave than I expected." He looked nervous. "And if you will excuse me," he said to both of them, "I must go." He turned on his heel and walked away from the small crowd and across the street.

"A slave auction? That's horrendous!" said Sera. "Come on. We need to see what's happening. Maybe this is why we landed here."

Dak shrugged and followed Sera as she weaved her way through the crowd.

Soon, a voice rose higher than all the others, and the crowd hushed. "Welcome!" the man said. "Attention! Take a close look at these fine slaves and get your bids ready. We've a prime young woman laborer with two children, not to be split. Think potential. A boy around six and an infant girl, two generations of work for the price of one. And we have a strong young man around sixteen, suitable for hard labor or household work. Last chance to examine them is now. Bidding begins in thirty minutes!"

Sera and Dak pushed to the front, much to the annoyance of the adults who were waiting to get a closer look at the slaves. Finally, Dak made it around the bulk of the townspeople and found an open space off to the side. He looked over at the short makeshift platform in front of the courthouse, and then he gasped.

"Gorgonzola milquetoast!" he cried, turning to Sera. "It's Riq!"

Kissy Bowley

RIQ READ the flyer again as he and Kessiah stood on the platform for viewing. It was a distraction from all the eyes that were on him. The first time he read it, his attention had been drawn to his own name, spelled in the style of the era, but something else stuck out, too. The flyer said the woman's name was Kissy.

"Kessiah," Riq whispered. They were chained together at the ankles now, and their hands were free.

She just barely tilted her head, indicating she was listening.

"The flyer says your name is Kissy Bowley. Is it really Kissy?"

"Folks call me Kissy. Kessiah is my given name."

Riq was quiet for a moment. How could he ask her without sounding odd? "Do you have an aunt, by any chance?"

"I have about a dozen aunts."

Riq shoved his hands in his pockets and looked out at the sea of mostly white faces scrutinizing him. He wanted to kick each and every one of them. "Aunt Minty?" He said it so softly that he wasn't sure she heard him.

"Who are you?" she asked, her tone suspicious.

"I'm—" Riq squeezed his eyes shut as a Remnant of cold nothingness socked him in the chest. He couldn't finish the sentence. He didn't know what to say.

"Who are you?" she demanded. "How do you know my aunt?"

Riq hazarded a glance and caught her eye. He tried again. "I'm—I think we're . . . related."

"Quiet down," one of the handlers said, poking Riq in the back with a stick or a cane or something.

He didn't dare speak again.

∞

Sera stared. There was Riq, standing on the wooden platform, shoulders uncharacteristically sloped forward, and a look of emptiness on his face that pierced through Sera's gut. "What on earth?" she muttered. And then she stomped over to the front of the crowd. "Out of my way," she said whenever anyone tried to stop her. "That young man is not a slave."

"Sera!" Dak cried, and then he went charging after her. When he reached her, he whispered, "I know what's happening here is way wrong, but we can*not* mess this up, so don't blow a gasket in public, okay? We don't need to make things worse for Riq, and we don't need a bunch of SQ figuring us out. I'm sure Bigmouth Beeson has already informed them—"

By this time they had reached the front of the throng. A simple rope separated them from the people on the platform, and Sera saw that Riq was shackled to the woman next to him. Sera pushed in against the rope as far as she could go so that she was only a few feet away from him and no one stood next to her.

"Riq," she said in a harsh whisper.

He lifted his head. At the sight of her and Dak, Riq's lips parted slightly, then he closed them again. His eyelids closed for a long second, and he took in a deep breath and let it out slowly. When he opened them again, he looked directly into Sera's eyes. She could see his were swimming. He pressed his lips together and looked away.

Sera studied him. "Oh, no—they broke your nose?" Her bread-to-the-face incident seemed embarrassingly minor compared to this. She felt heat rising from her neck for having made such a big deal about it. When Riq didn't answer her, she set her jaw and muttered to Dak over her shoulder, "He's not allowed to talk to us." Angry tears came to her eyes. "This is so wrong."

"It's awful," Dak said. "We need to get him out of here. But we have to play it smart." He nodded toward the big men roaming the area, looking like they wanted to pound and slice anybody who ventured too close to them or the slaves.

Sera fingered the lapels of the coat she so desperately wanted to give back to Riq, but she wasn't sure what would happen if she did it—there were five burly men surrounding the platform, and she didn't want anybody to get in trouble. Especially Riq.

She dropped her hands and clenched them at her sides. "Where on earth are the people who can help us?" she whispered to Dak. "There has to be someone who can help." She looked around. The slave woman lifted her head and caught Sera's eye, and then immediately shifted her gaze to a spot in the distance. She remained staring at it, unmoving.

"Did she hear me?" Sera whispered to Dak. She watched the woman gaze steadily, and then Sera slowly turned to look over her shoulder. All she could see was an angry-looking man's giant nostrils and bloodshot eyes. She looked up higher, above his head, and saw a squat steeple across the street.

Sera smiled politely at the man, then slowly turned back to face the podium. "The church?" she whispered.

Sera thought she saw the woman nod, but it was so slight that Sera couldn't tell for sure. However, she was certain the woman didn't shake her head no, so she supposed her hunch was correct.

The crowd pushed in on Sera, and she strained against the rope, trying to come up with a plan before anyone pushed her aside. Dak began to chatter with people behind Sera, and she could tell he was distracting them purposely. She looked at Riq one last time, wishing he wasn't tethered to the woman. This would be one time she'd be willing to use the Infinity Ring to warp the three of them out of here, but she couldn't very well take the woman and baby with her, leaving the little boy standing here alone—that would be terrible. The poor little boy would never get over it.

"We'll get you out of here," Sera whispered to Riq. Her tone was confident, but at the moment, she had not one single idea how she would keep her promise.

Riq didn't react. He just swallowed hard and kept his eyes to the ground.

14

Where the Crud Are the Hystorians?

SERA AND Dak left their spot in front of the courthouse steps and pushed to the outskirts of the crowd so they could talk without a bunch of rotten slave buyers breathing down their necks. "Where the crud are the Hystorians?" Dak asked when they finally had some space.

Sera smacked him right in the SQuare. "According to the clue," she said, "they're either at the post office or some guy named Gourdon will lead us to one. I don't know."

"But it's never taken us this long to find help before. And we even speak this language!"

Sera glanced down the block and across the street to the little church that the woman—whose name was Kissy according to the auction sign—had stared at. "We don't have time to run there now before the auction starts. We can't let Riq out of our sight."

"The clue says we need the post office, not the church."

Sera worked the edges of her shawl, her eyes darting this way and that. "I know," she said. "But did you see her look up when she heard me say we needed help?"

"You mean like Mrs. Fake SQuaker woman did?" Dak was skeptical. "Something very fishy is happening."

The dark-skinned Quaker man that Dak had talked to earlier now walked back toward them from across the street, returning from wherever he'd gone. He was singing a song, and when he reached them, he gave them a meaningful look.

"Sir?" Dak said.

The man stopped. "How can I help thee?"

"Where's the post office?"

"There's no post office in Cambridge."

Dak stared at him. "Well, where's the nearest one?"

The man raised a finger to his lips, drawing it over his mustache in a contemplative manner. "You're not from around here, are you, children?"

"No," Sera butted in. "We're not." She gave him a long look.

He nodded slowly and a smile played at the corner of his mouth. "I see. I reckon the post office you're looking for is in that church, then."

Dak and Sera looked at each other, and then back at the man.

"Nobody's there to help you now, though. Probably not until this afternoon." He tipped his hat and began to walk away.

"Thank you," Sera called out after him. "Sir?"

He turned.

"Is your name Gourdon?"

He looked puzzled. "No, miss. It's John. John Bowley." He nodded one last time and walked back to the auction area, singing once again.

"I think he's on our side," Dak said.

"But why didn't he say anything?"

"Maybe he's not sure about us."

"At this point, I'm not sure about anything," Sera said. "SQ posing as Quakers? Inviting runaways in and then capturing them, and selling them back to plantations? Keeping people working against their will and treating them like dirt? Why, Dak?"

"Think about it," Dak said. "Plantation owners have a lot of land to farm—more than they can handle on their own. So they buy a slave and they get them for life, or however long they want them. They don't have to pay wages day in and day out. When a slave runs away or gets set free, the plantation owner feels like they lost money. They have to buy another slave."

Sera exploded. "They shouldn't buy slaves at all! They should hire people and pay them! Not force them against their will!"

"I *know* that, Sera, but you asked for an explanation. I didn't say it was right, and I don't think it's right. But if you're wondering *why* plantation owners want to keep slaves from escaping or keep the government from freeing them, well, that's why. Money."

"So they don't see it as immoral," Sera said. "They see it as good business."

Dak nodded. "And the SQ has chosen their side. Not exactly surprising, since there's money *and* power at stake. They can't resist the chance to keep people down. Who knows what would happen if slaves were able to escape and work with the abolitionists? But now, everyone is scattered. The Fugitive Slave Act is scaring people who might want to help runaways. Slaves get punished if they talk to anyone. 'Without communication there can be no collaboration,'" he said, taking a quote often used by his father—although his father had used it when talking about household chores.

"So, putting it scientifically, you're saying the effort can't grow at a high enough rate of speed to produce the momentum necessary to change the country," Sera mused, and then she squeezed his arm and said, "You're really smart. That makes a lot of sense. You know, Dak, you can be so mature when you want to be."

Dak raised an eyebrow. "Like a fine cheese, I get better with age."

"And smellier," added Sera.

Just then, the ominous voice of the auctioneer rose from the front of the courthouse once again. "Let the bidding begin!"

15

The Bidding Begins

RIQ STOOD stone-faced and scared to death as a crowd of strangers stared at him, unsmiling, sizing him up. A handsome dark-skinned man in Quaker dress, with a hat pulled low over his eyes, was one of few black people in the crowd of what Riq assumed were plantation owners and slave traders. The man came up to peer at Riq and Kessiah.

The little boy, James, pointed at the man, but Kessiah shushed him, and he was quiet. The man looked solemnly at Kessiah for a long moment, and then smiled at the boy and winked, and then nodded as if he was satisfied. As he walked away, he began to hum to himself. The tune was familiar, and it didn't take Riq long to recognize the song that Kessiah had sung that morning along with women outside the window. *Run, mourner, run.*

Riq looked at Kessiah from the corner of his eye and watched as her entire body seemed to relax. She let out a light shuddering breath and inhaled deeply. She raised her head and faced the menacing-looking crowd with an air of confidence.

When the handlers took the shackles off for the bidding, the woman bent down, pretending to move the chain. Riq bent down, too, to help, since she held the infant tirelessly in one arm. "When things heat up, don't fight," she whispered. "Just run."

Riq's eyes opened up in alarm. "Where?"

"Get to the Choptank River and hide in the woods until dark. I can meet you there. But watch out—Bradshaw's Hotel is along the way."

Riq didn't know what Bradshaw's Hotel was, but it didn't sound good. "My friends won't know where I'm going," he whispered.

"Nothing I can do about that," Kessiah said, standing up. It wasn't unkind; it was just a fact.

Riq stood, too, and as he heard the auctioneer and saw his friends running toward the crowd, he wished either Dak or Sera knew sign language. All he could do was hope they didn't mess this up.

∞

"This is insane," Sera muttered for the second time in a day. Hands popped up all around when the bidding began for Riq at twenty-five dollars. "How much money do you have?"

"Five hundred and sixty-three dollars and forty-six cents."

Sera gripped his arm. "Are you serious?"

"Sure. It's in my college fund at home."

Sera sighed. "I mean how much with you? I've got six dollars and twenty-five cents."

Dak shook his head. "Nada." He paused. "Hey! That's three languages."

"Still too soon, Dak."

"Roger that."

"So," Sera said after a minute, "I'm thinking we just watch to see who wins the auction, and follow that person home. Do you have any other ideas?"

"We could rush the stage, grab him, and warp out of here."

"Yeah, those enormous constables or handlers or whatever they're called won't mind. I'm sure they've never seen anybody try anything at a slave auction before."

"Maybe you could change the inflection in your voice just a little more when you say things like that, because I might miss the sarcasm," Dak said.

"*Yeaaaah,* those *enooooormous* constables—"

"Quiet—I think the bidding is slowing down. And look, the beefy dudes are all bored looking—there's only one watching Riq." Dak looked at Sera.

"Are you thinking what I'm thinking?"

"Yeah. Let's go."

Finally, only two bidders remained. And then one. The auctioneer slammed his hand down on his podium, making Riq jump. He looked out to the crowd to see who had bought him. Even though Kessiah had assured him something was going to happen, he didn't know what or when. Or if it even really included him. All he knew was that he was no longer free, and someone now owned him.

It was the worst feeling in the world. Even worse than the Remnants.

And then he remembered how Kissy's story went.

16

Escape

WITH KESSIAH now on the block, Riq's heart sank. As he recalled the story Grandma Phoebe had told him, great-great-great-great-grandmother Kissy, along with her children, had been auctioned. Her husband, who was free, tried to buy her freedom, but failed. They attempted escape, but failed at that, too. And Kissy never saw John again.

And now the man who little James had pointed at was bidding. Suddenly it all made sense, and Riq was the only one who knew it was going to fail.

Another near-nauseating Remnant shook Riq's existence—and his confidence. And he knew, now. He knew it for certain. His Remnants were not at all like Sera's Remnants. That's why he couldn't share descriptions with her back when they were with the Vikings in the year 911. When he'd told her they were nothing—he'd meant it literally. That's exactly what they were. A nothingness so black, cold, and void of any kind of love . . . there was nothing more *nothing* than that.

While Sera's Remnants were the ache of love between people, of a life that could have been, his were the helpless ache of suffocation, the shocking ache of a body plunged into ice water. The harsh ache of bone scraping bone.

And to Riq, after years of pondering the phenomenon, it could mean only one thing: He wasn't supposed to be here. He wasn't supposed to exist.

If he let things happen as they did, with John failing to rescue his family, with them never seeing one another again, then Kissy would eventually start a new family—a family that would one day include Riq. But what if he intervened? Maybe he could keep John and Kissy together and ensure James grew up in freedom. Maybe he could help them find Aunt Minty, who was somehow sabotaged in her efforts to save them. Maybe that was exactly what he was supposed to do to fix the Break.

Even if it meant he would never be born.

Just then the auctioneer's hand slammed down once again and Kessiah was sold to John Bowley. Her husband. Just the way his grandmother had told him. There was a murmur in the crowd as people realized a freedman had just won a slave auction. This sort of thing wasn't supposed to happen, and the people were beginning to react.

Riq wasn't sure what would come next, but what he didn't expect to see was Dak and Sera, running toward him, holding out the Infinity Ring.

"Grab on!" Dak shouted.

Riq shook his head in disbelief. As much as he wanted to, he couldn't abandon this mission now. "No!" he cried. "Don't touch me!" He dodged around them and took off running. His shouting alerted the handlers, who turned their attention from the restless crowd back to Riq.

∞

Dak and Sera stood speechless, caught completely off guard by Riq's reaction to their rescue attempt. They watched as he ran down the courthouse steps and the five guards gave pursuit. Kissy, meanwhile, wasted no time. She pushed her son into John Bowley's arms, then, cradling her baby to her chest, leapt off the steps and disappeared into the crowd.

"Come on!" Dak cried, taking off after the guards. "We can't lost sight of Riq!"

"I know!" Sera hollered back. "But it's hard to run in this muumuu!"

"Just try and keep up!"

"Just try wearing a dress," Sera said back at him, but not as loud. "Look!" she called. "He's circling around. We need to cut the big guys off so he can get away. This way!" She veered off toward the church/post office/whatever it was, and Dak doubled back and followed her. "You take the far one, I'll hit the close one, and with any luck—"

Dak waved his arm to shush her as Riq ran past. "Sanctuary!" Dak yelled to Riq when he went by, and then he crossed in front of one guard, tripping him, and tackled another. Sera jumped onto the back of a third, whipped her shawl off her shoulders, and pulled it tight around the guard's neck. The other two guards hesitated, waiting for instructions from their fallen leader, which gave Riq just enough time to snake around an outbuilding and into the woods.

The guard Dak had tackled shoved Dak off of himself and started running again, while Sera's guard fell to his knees, gasping for air and slapping at Sera's legs. As soon as she could safely hop off, she did, leaving a nasty rope-like burn around the guard's neck as she pulled her shawl free. She gave him a final kick with her boot between his shoulder blades, grabbed Dak's hand to pull him to his feet, and then they headed in the opposite direction, so filled with fear and adrenaline that they didn't look back until they had made it all the way to the wooded lot behind the church. They stopped to catch their breaths, realizing that exactly nobody had followed them.

They high-fived behind a gorgeous sassafras tree, and then the accolades, complete with various accents, began.

"We're the Two Musketeers!"

"No, we're Inigo Montoya!"

"No, we're the Incredible-ests!"

"No, we're the Count!"

"Wait, what?"

"The Count!"

"The Count of what?"

"You know, that one guy. Who was really tough and vengeful and stuff."

"Oh. Um, no, I guess I don't know."

"They named a sandwich after him or something."

"You mean the Earl of Sandwich?"

"No, I'm quite sure it was a count. . . ."

"Well, in any case. We rock."

"We roll!"

They both looked around.

"But we still don't have Riq."

"Riq rolls!"

"Right."

There was a brief pause to account for waning enthusiasm.

Sera sighed. "I hope he knew what you meant when you yelled 'sanctuary.'"

"I meant 'church.' Who wouldn't know that?"

"Hopefully the guards wouldn't, because I'm sure they heard, too," Sera said.

"Oh. Well, yes. But they can't get us if we're in the church, though, can they? Isn't that against the rules?"

"Only if it's really a church and not a post office. And only if we're in the movies."

"That? Is next on the agenda to figure out."

"You need to figure out if we're in the movies? If so, we're in a sorry state indeed."

"No, the post-office-in-the-church part."

"Well, that's a relief. Shall we, then?"

"We shall."

Sera slipped her hand in the crook of Dak's elbow, which made him stand all stiff and weird, because he'd done that once before when he was the ring bearer at his aunt Tricia's wedding and he had to escort some little crying girl down the aisle and throw the stupid flower petals for her because some strange wart-faced old woman hissed at him to do it at the last second. Dak shook his head in disgust, remembering. Parents really had no idea what psychological issues they caused, making their kids do such horrible things.

Anyway, Dak pulled his arm away, Sera shrugged and picked up her dress instead so it didn't drag on the squishy, moist peat and wet grass, and they snuck in the back door of the church.

Down by the River

RIQ FELT like he could run forever. It was a kamikaze mission, after all—what did he have to lose besides his own existence? His heart lifted as he zigzagged around the bumbling guards, loping along at a very comfortable pace for a guy who'd played halfback in soccer for the past seven years—not that his parents had ever taken the time to see him play. And while his broken nose throbbed, his focus was on leading the men farther and farther away from the river so he could lose them for good.

If only he could get word to the church, to Dak and Sera, that he wouldn't be making it there to meet them. Perhaps there was a way to do so—he wasn't sure. But he also remembered the clue, and he hoped that they would do what they'd all promised one another they'd do: complete the mission. Complete the mission. Complete the mission. It was more important than anything else in the universe. It was so important that it was absolutely, well, cataclysmic.

While he'd stood on that podium, Riq had deduced that the five burly men were probably SQ agents who didn't recognize him for what he really was—even though their job with the SQ required them to be on guard for the organization's enemies. Because they were too busy being blinded by his skin color, they failed to realize that he was a Hystorian. Well, Riq decided, perhaps he would just have to use that to his advantage.

Now, a good three miles into the woods, he led them on the chase in zigzag fashion. When they started to lag and he knew not only that he could get away, but also that they wouldn't make it to the Choptank River anytime soon, he jumped into a small stream, stopped, and started running through it, back the way he'd come. His footprints in this damp soil would be too easy to track, but the water would fix that. So he jogged all the way downstream to where he could see the town again, from a different side this time. Once he got his bearings, he stepped onto the grass, pulled his hat down over his eyes, and tried to look like he was running errands. He kept his head down and didn't look anybody with light-colored skin in the eye.

He saw a bustling hotel from the back side and got past it without incident, and then continued on to the Choptank River. There were small ships and oyster boats all along the wharf, up to where the docks met the woods. Riq headed that way, unsure what to do next except hide until dark—this was as much information as Kessiah had been able to give him. But he definitely had to wait for her. He hadn't figured out all the pieces yet, but between the clues in the SQuare and the evidence of his own Remnants, it seemed Kissy and her family were caught up in the SQ's plot.

He told himself it all came down to the mission. But this time, it was personal. He absolutely had to see to the family's—his family's—safety. No matter what happened along the way—and no matter the consequences.

18

The Postman Delivers

DAK AND Sera burst through the door of the church and looked around, expecting to see some sort of activity. But there was no one there at all. The afternoon sun streamed in, giving the church not only light but a bit of warmth as well.

"So, where's the post office?" Dak asked.

Sera looked around. "And where's Riq?"

"You know," Dak mused, "isn't it kind of illegal to have a post office in a church? Thomas Jefferson often spoke against the mingling of church affairs with those of the government, and the post office is a government institution."

Sera shrugged, not really caring.

"Then again," Dak continued, "Thomas Jefferson also said all men are created equal, and even put it in the Declaration of Independence. Yet he owned slaves. That doesn't seem quite right either. There was this one English guy, an abolitionist back then, who said something like 'there's nothing more absurd than an important dude signing something saying everybody's the same with one hand while holding a slave whip in the other hand.'"

Sera squinted at Dak. "English guy had a point." She looked around the church. It was simple and sparse. "So," she said, "if this is the post office, where's the mail?" She began to look in earnest. "Maybe it's hidden."

Dak shot her a quizzical look, and then frowned to himself as if he were deep in thought. Then he said, "I wonder . . ." He didn't continue speaking. Instead he went up to the front of the church where the minister would stand, behind a wooden pulpit. He knelt down, feeling all around the base of it.

"What are you doing?" Sera called from the back of the church.

"Looking for mail. I think you might be on the right track. I just remembered something—slaves weren't really allowed to talk to each other or gather together much when they were working. But they could go to church on Sunday, and that's where—" Dak heard a noise, which echoed in the near-vacant building.

Sera whirled around. "Who's there?" she said, trying to sound calm. She scrambled to her feet.

A man with a heavy beard rounded the corner into the sanctuary near Sera and stopped. "Oh, good afternoon," he said. He held a package under his arm, which he deftly slipped inside his suit jacket.

"Hello," Sera said, noting his swift move. She decided

not to speak, knowing that if she didn't offer any information about herself, that meant the man had to ask for it, which put her in a better position. Perhaps he'd offer information willingly. She tilted her head, as if she expected him to.

"I'm Gamaliel Bailey," the man said. "Are you two lost? Looking for something, perhaps?"

"Why would you think we're lost?" Sera demanded.

The man took a step back and held up his hands. "I apologize and meant nothing by the statement. Since this is a black church, it surprised me to see you two here. Has your nanny brought you here?"

Sera's mouth opened. "No," she said in an icy voice. "We don't have a nanny, thank you. And you're not black either," she pointed out.

The man pursed his lips. "You must live nearby, then?"

"No," Sera said.

"Yes," Dak said at the same time.

The man struggled to hide a smile. "I see."

"Are you the minister?" Dak asked. He glared at Sera, who glared back at him.

"Good heavens, no," he said with a laugh. "I'm a physician-turned-newspaper-editor, I suppose. I run a little paper called the *National Era* in Washington, DC, and—"

"Wait a second—that's where Harriet Beecher Stowe's book was first published! It's an abolitionist paper," Dak said to Sera.

The man looked confused. "Which book?"

"Uncle Tom's Cabin," Dak said, triumphant that he finally got something right about this history. "Starting in 1851."

Sera's face froze, her eyes wide.

Dak froze, too.

Gamaliel Bailey's lips parted and then closed again. His face grew thoughtful, and then a look of wonder passed over it. His eyes began to shine and he sniffed once, putting a loose fist to his mouth as if he were going to cough, but he didn't cough, he just held it there for a long moment.

"I mean . . ." Dak said in a quiet voice, "it was probably a different paper in eighteen-Sasquach or something."

A grin spread over Gamaliel's face at that, and he dropped his fist from his mouth and clasped his fingers together. He stood, gazing at the children, his head shaking the slightest bit from side to side, as if he couldn't believe what he was seeing. Finally, he came to his senses.

"Welcome," he said. "I never thought I'd see you. Never in a thousand years. And"—his eyes grew misty—"I can't tell you how much we need you right now." He pointed to a pew. "Do you have time to sit down and talk? I'm a Hystorian. This isn't my post—I'm normally in Washington, DC, but there's been a bit of trouble here lately, so I came down to help."

Sera frowned. She was skeptical of everyone in this period. She crossed her arms. "How do we know you're really a Hystorian? Prove it."

The man didn't look surprised at all by the question.

It was as if he'd been waiting his whole life to answer it. He spoke in low tones. "In 336 BC, the most amazing visionary, Aristotle, foresaw that the world was headed toward a great danger. The true course of history was being broken, and he realized it would continue well after he was gone. But he also predicted that someday, people would be able to travel back in time and fix the Breaks in history. He established a secret group called the Hystorians to watch for the time travelers. I have been one for many years, as were my parents before me."

Sera narrowed her eyes. "So, you're friends with Mrs. Beeson," she said. Not a question.

His eyes hardened. "Yes, Mrs. Beeson is a wonderful woman, and a steadfast abolitionist. She is, however, missing." He dropped his gaze. "Many brave people along the Freedom Trail from here to Philadelphia are missing. My comrades and friends. That's why I've come to help." He wiped his face with his hand, holding it over his eyes for a moment. "Everything we've worked for all these years is in jeopardy. My paper has been attacked, and I'm being violently forced out of business." He looked at Dak. "As a matter of fact, Ms. Stowe wrote to me recently to inform me that she was hoping to provide a work of fiction for my paper. But the way things look now, there won't be anything at all printed in the *National Era* in 1851, because it won't exist."

He pulled the package from his jacket pocket and tossed it to the seat next to him. "Letters," he said. "Coded letters for the slaves from their free friends and family. Letters from stations on the Underground Railroad, and from conductors who are planning their next runs. We hide them here—it's the only safe place for the slaves to get communication." He looked up at Sera and Dak. "These letters and I nearly didn't make it here today."

Just then his face paled to ash and he cringed. He grabbed hold of the bench and held his breath, as if in pain.

"Are you all right?" Sera asked. She stood up and gave a helpless look around, unsure what to do.

The man shook his head and held up a hand. When he could speak, he said, "Don't be afraid. I've been having some strange episodes lately—like flashes of memories, but memories of things I don't quite remember. I know it doesn't make sense. Perhaps in the future, there's a cure for such things." He looked up, hopeful, but when he saw the look on Sera's face, the smile faded dead away.

19

The Real Deal This Time

"I GUESS you could say we're working on a cure," Sera said. "They're called Remnants." She looked at her hands.

Dak nodded, even though he didn't fully understand what they were talking about. He hadn't ever experienced a Remnant, but he knew Sera and Riq both had them, as well as countless other people. And speaking of Riq . . . "Would you excuse us for a moment please, Dr. Bailey?"

"Of course."

Dak pulled Sera down the aisle to the front of the church. "I just wanted to make sure you think he's the real deal before I stick my stupid foot in my even stupider mouth again."

Sera bumped the toe of his boot with the toe of hers. "What, 1851? It turned out fine," she said. "You big dope."

He grinned, feeling loads better now. "So, do we believe his story?"

"I think we do. Do we?"

"Yes. And maybe next time we'll be smart enough not to believe every person who tells us they're on our side."

"We can't be perfect every second of the day," Sera said. "Okay. Let's trust him."

"And then," Dak said, peering outside through the windows at the late afternoon sunset, "we really need to find Riq and that Gourdon guy."

"Riq should be here by now," Sera said. "Maybe he didn't know the meaning of . . ." She trailed off with an embarrassed smile. "Oh, yeah. Linguist."

"I thought it was too soon for linguist jokes."

"Stop it. Let's go."

They returned to Gamaliel Bailey, and Dak spoke up. "So, if you're sure you're feeling all right, we need to start looking for our friend Riq, who is also a time traveler. He was captured last night by the imposter Mrs. Beeson, and sold as a slave today, which really messed up everything, even though he escaped. I'm sure fake Mrs. Beeson is not as lovely as the real one."

"Oh, dear, that's terrible," Gamaliel said, standing up and wringing his hands. "I'm here to help you, though, and I will do everything I can."

"We also need to wait here for a bit, then find and follow some drinking guy named Gourdon. Any chance you know him?"

"Gourdon? I know of no such man, I fear, but you'll remember I'm not from here. You're to follow him, you say?"

"Yes, but we also need to find Riq." Dak was beginning to get anxious. "I hope he hasn't been captured again."

Gamaliel Bailey lifted a finger as if to speak, then held the pose for a moment, a puzzled look on his face. "Forgive me, children—I'm replaying our conversation in my mind—did you say you were to follow a drinking man named Gourdon?"

Sera raised an eyebrow at Dak, then turned back to the man. "Yes," she said.

"*Hmm.* Can you tell me your instructions exactly?"

Sera tapped her finger against her thigh as she rattled off, "Seek not lantern or Friends. After tomorrow's fair, visit post office. Wait, then follow the drinking Gourdon."

Gamaliel almost smiled, but he still had a puzzled look on his face. "Was it in clue form?"

"Yes, it was set up like a telegram sent from Gourdon."

The man chuckled, and then his laugh grew louder and louder. "Oh," he said. "Oh, my. I surely needed that today. Gourdon, indeed."

Sera and Dak looked at each other as if poor Gamaliel had lost his marbles.

"Children, it's not a man you seek. It's a constellation. I'm sure signing the telegram with the word *gourd* would have been too obvious, so I imagine your guide was being clever. Can you guess which constellation looks a bit like a drinking gourd?"

Dak knew astronomy was Sera's weakest science. And he didn't have a clue what a drinking gourd looked like, so he was no help.

When neither answered, Gamaliel said, "A drinking gourd is the hollowed-out bottom half of a gourd, which is sometimes used as a cup. Attached to the gourd is a stick, several inches long, so that if you leave the gourd in a pail of drinking water, the handle sticks out above the surface so you can grab hold, or use it as a *dipper*." He emphasized the last word.

"*Ooh*, I get it," Sera said. "This is an easy one. The Drinking Gourd is the Big Dipper."

"And the Big Dipper points the way to . . . ?"

"The North Star," Dak said.

"Your clue said to wait," Gamaliel said. "Probably until the stars come out."

"And then we follow the Drinking Gourd . . . but where?" Sera said. She didn't like dealing with such vague instructions.

"Sera," Dak said in a very serious voice, "Dr. Bailey said abolitionists are missing from here to Philadelphia. We saw for ourselves that the SQ is responsible. So we need to go north. We'll follow the Freedom Trail, flush out the phony abolitionists, and find the *real* abolitionists so that they can continue to help runaways and work toward freedom and equality."

Gamaliel stood, hat in hand. "As it stands now, the plantation owners are winning against us abolitionists. They're using more and more violent means to stop us. My newspaper has been threatened, and so has my life. I will fight to the end to keep my paper going, but I'm afraid if they get rid of me, no one else will dare to step in. It's very dangerous." He turned to Dak. "Your mention of something I'll publish in the new year gives me great hope that I'll survive at least a bit longer. But who knows what will happen after that?" And then he paused and frowned. "Well, I guess you do."

"A war," Sera whispered. "That's what happens. And it lasts forever."

Gamaliel looked as though he didn't dare ask if *forever* was an exaggeration.

Dak sucked in a breath and blew it out. Things were getting intense. "Well, if we don't have to stay here to wait for the drunk dude," he said, laughing a little, because now it sounded really ridiculous, "somebody should go find Riq."

"I'll do it," Sera said. "You stay here in case he comes after all. He had the clue, too, remember? He figured it out, so I bet if he's not captured again, he'll know that we've all got to follow the Drinking Gourd." She looked around the church for a clock, with no luck. "Don't go anywhere," she said. "I'll be back a little after dark whether I've found him or not. And then we'll figure out what to do next."

With that, she was gone. A moment later, Dak and Gamaliel saw her bonneted head bobbing up and down as she ran down the street, clutching the shawl around her neck in one hand and holding Riq's coat in the other.

"She's a spunky girl," the man said.

"All the girls are like that in our time." Dak grimaced.

Gamaliel smiled warmly. "Good. There's hope, then,

for all. That gives me more joy than you know."

When Sera had disappeared from sight, Dak turned back to the Hystorian. "How do we follow the Drinking Gourd, exactly? The sky is so vast. Are there trails, or do you just sort of . . . go north?"

"The way to freedom here along the coast," Gamaliel said, "is to go to the water, but there are no set trails. Most runaways have to make it out on their wits alone, or with a bit of help from other slaves or freedmen, and the occasional pale-skinned abolitionist who has no qualms about breaking the law. But we're lucky here—the Choptank River is just a few blocks away. It feeds into the Chesapeake Bay. Until about a week ago or so, runaway slaves were sometimes able to escape with a sympathetic sailor and get as far as Baltimore, at least."

"But not now?"

"Not now. Not safely, anyway. With all of the SQ posing as kind, good-hearted abolitionists, luring runaways into their homes and ships to capture and sell them again, there's no way to know whom to trust. It's chaos. We desperately need to get our Hystorians back and restore the system, or else no one will ever hear of the Underground Railroad." His face was solemn.

Dak didn't have the heart to tell him that in their time, no one but the geekiest historians had ever heard of it, and they knew it as a failure.

20

Finding Riq

SERA RAN from one end of town to the other, which took almost no time at all in a town that didn't even have a post office. She poked her head inside a tavern, wrinkled up her nose, and backed out again. Riq wouldn't be in there. She slipped into Bradshaw's Hotel, where a group of men stood in a circle talking about buying and selling slaves and how much money they were making these days thanks to the Fugitive Slave Act, which they called the Bloodhound Law.

She wandered past them and stood nearby with her back to them, pretending to wait for someone, and they took no notice of her at all. She saw the fake Mrs. Beeson slip into the hotel, and that was enough to make Sera circle the group and exit in a hurry. She didn't see Riq anywhere, so reluctantly she left and turned toward the Choptank River wharf.

Since it was December, she was surprised to see so much activity by the water. The air was brisk. Sera pulled her shawl tighter around her shoulders and scanned the various boats as daylight disappeared. She was getting anxious. She decided that Riq wouldn't be milling around on the road after what had happened earlier, so she took a very long walk in a roundabout way along the river behind the village shops, following a small stream into the edge of the woods on her way back toward the church. And that's where she spied a young man sitting with his back against a tree.

She moved closer. "Riq?"

He scrambled to his feet and whirled around. "Sera," he said. "Wow. You scared me. I'm so glad to see you."

She ran up to him. "Why didn't you come to the church? Didn't you hear Dak?"

"I heard him. But I couldn't. I can't. There are slave traders *everywhere*. I couldn't risk crossing the street after what happened earlier—everybody knows what I look like."

"Well, it's getting dark now. Can you come with me? We'll sneak across."

He sighed deeply. "It's not just the risk," he admitted. "It's . . . well, I'm supposed to meet Kessiah here. See, I found out a bunch of stuff. She's related to me, and . . ."

Sera stared. "She's what?"

"She's my great-great-something-grandmother. I know it's crazy, but I'm telling you, being up on that platform was like déjà vu—I'd heard the story of that auction so many times from my grandma Phoebe. . . . I didn't even realize. It was just so strange and awful, but somehow it was amazing because she's, you know, my family."

Sera gazed up at him, wishing she really did understand. "Does she know that?"

"No. But I know something's weird, and I know from my grandma that something bad happens, and I think it all has to do with the Break. I need to stay with Kessiah. I need to make sure she stays safe. It—" He hesitated, then said in a very quiet voice, "It has something to do with my Remnants, Sera." He left it at that, and Sera knew better than to press him for more details. "We're bound for Baltimore. And that's the same way you guys have to go, too, according to the clue—you got the Drinking Gourd reference, right?"

"Um," Sera said in a breezy manner, "oh yeah, sure, right away. Easy one. Yep."

He grinned. "I knew you'd get it eventually. Did you find the Hystorian? The real one, I mean?"

"We found *a* Hystorian, yes. He's very nice."

"Good." He dug the toe of his boot in the mud, thinking. "Okay, then. Here's my plan. I'm going with Kissy and John tonight—she's a runaway, and he's a fugitive for taking them, so we're all on the run—and I'm going to keep them safe until we meet Aunt Minty in Baltimore. She's supposed to take them farther north, but something goes wrong along the way. Something I may be able to help with. So," he said, "I will meet you guys in Baltimore, and we'll figure out a plan from there." He waited, not breathing, for her response.

Her face wrinkled up. "But, Riq," she said, "no. Just . . . no. We need you, and I hate when we're all split up. It makes me really nervous. How far is Baltimore from here?"

"It's north, up the Chesapeake Bay, like seventy-five miles. You guys can take land, and I'll take the water where it's safer. Okay? Please?" He jiggled his foot with nervous energy.

She looked skeptical.

Riq sighed. "Remember when we were in the 885 Break and Dak was desperate to experience a Viking ship because he's so in love with history and it was the chance of a lifetime, and so we said fine, go ahead? This is like that. This is my Viking ship." He grabbed her hand and looked into her eyes. "Please, Sera."

She flushed in the dark and looked down. "Yeah, okay, I get that, but look at the trouble Dak made because of his once-in-a-lifetime opportunity. He could have died. Or one of us, trying to rescue him."

"Yes, but there's no war here!" He bit his lip, knowing he was too loud, and lowered his voice. "There's no war, no projectile missiles or boiling oil raining down. It's just a simple overnight ride up the bay." His eyes begged her as the stars began to pop in the night sky.

"Why can't you wait for me to get Dak and the Hystorian so we can all go together?"

"We're too big a group. The only way this will work is if we can avoid drawing attention. And besides, you two need to focus on the mission. Keeping Kissy safe is just one part of that."

"Grrr," Sera said. It was getting late. She had to get back to the church.

They heard a noise and tensed, on their guard, but it was Kessiah and John and the children. James, in his father's arms, clutched a blanket.

"Riq," Kessiah whispered. "It's time. We have to go." She nodded to Sera. "Thank you for causing that distraction," she said. "We'll always be grateful." Her eyes traveled downward to Riq's and Sera's hands clasped together, and her mouth opened, then closed again. But then she controlled her expression and turned back to Riq. In a more sympathetic voice, she said, "I'm sorry. We need to make it to Federal Hill by late morning. If we're not there in time . . ." She didn't finish the sentence, but everyone knew what she meant.

Riq turned back to Sera. "Please."

Sera looked from Kessiah to John to Riq, closed her eyes, leaned back against the tree, and sighed. Kessiah and John both nodded their good-byes to Sera and turned to go.

Sera pulled her hand from Riq's and picked up the Quaker jacket, holding it out to him. "Here," she said. "Go. Stay safe, all of you. I don't know how long it'll take us to get there. . . ." She trailed off, hoping Gamaliel would know.

Riq took the jacket and surprised Sera by grabbing her in a tight bear hug, and whispered, "Thanks," in her ear. Then he added, "Federal Hill in Baltimore. I'll see you there tomorrow." He turned, taking a few steps to follow John and Kessiah. Then he paused and ran back to Sera, gripped her forearms, and looked wildly around.

"If something happens and we don't make it, or I don't make it, you know what you have to do. Promise me?"

Sera's lip quivered. "Nothing will happen to you." She stared at him, his gaze unwavering, waiting.

"If it does," he said urgently.

Finally, she nodded. "I promise," she whispered.

He turned and was gone into the night.

21

When Goons Attack

KESSIAH, CARRYING baby Araminta; John, walking with young James; and Riq picked their way in the dark along the small stream until it met the impressive Choptank River. John led them through the dark behind an oyster-shucking house, through a maze of giant piles of oyster shells, sneaking around them rather than taking the more populated walk along the wharf. Riq could smell the salty brine. There was a brisk breeze, but the stars were bright and there wasn't a cloud in the sky that he could see.

"We can watch from here," John said, crouching down. He glanced at Riq, sizing him up. "We're waiting for an oyster boat. It's small, but I pray we all fit."

Riq knew who'd be left out if they didn't.

"With this wind," Kessiah said, "we'll make good time, won't we?"

"If it lasts." John, who worked as a ship's carpenter, held a finger to his lips as three hulking men came into view across the wharf. They wandered through the piles of shells as if they were looking for something.

A moment later, as a small oyster boat under sail glided toward the dock, the three men split up and began to circle the area twenty yards away.

John signaled to the crew in the boat, and one of them signaled back. Riq watched, waiting for his cue. He smiled at James, who somehow understood the seriousness of all of this and was quiet. But the baby . . .

Kessiah cradled the baby to her, but she began to fuss and cry. John's eyes widened in alarm. He turned his head toward the three men getting closer, and then he looked at Riq and Kessiah. They had to go—it was now or never. They'd have to risk being seen. "Be quick," he said. "You and the baby, then James and I will follow. Riq, you come after me."

Riq and Kessiah nodded. She gripped a small bag and the baby, and ran to the boat. The men in the boat helped her in, and then John began to run with young James, and that's when one of the three enormous men saw the movement.

"Stop!" the man hollered. "Who are you?" He came running, the other two on his heels.

"Go!" Riq yelled. He got up, ready to run but waiting, knowing he couldn't go until James and John were settled to make sure the boat didn't capsize.

The wind gusted, taking James's blanket with it.

"Hey!" James yelled. He turned to get it, pulling from his father's grasp just as they were about to step into the vessel. John, thrown off balance, nearly fell into the icy water, and instead twisted and fell hard on his back on the edge of the boat, managing to roll into it rather than into the water. He cried out, clutching his back, and writhed in pain. He was completely unable to go after James.

The slave hunters thundered toward the boat and the boy.

"James!" Riq cried, his stomach lurching. He tore after him, scooped up the blanket and James in one smooth move, and then whirled around, three angry men bearing down on him.

Kessiah screamed, baby Araminta wailed, John gasped and groaned, the stranger piloting the boat whipped his head around and yelled "Go!" and Riq—carrying James—tried desperately to dodge the men and make it into the boat, whispering, "Hang on to me!" into James's neck. But despite Kessiah's screams, the captain of the vessel pulled away for his own escape, and there was nowhere for Riq and James to go but into the frigid river, or back into the woods.

The Journey Begins

"THE GOOD news," Gamaliel said as he, Dak, and Sera made their way toward the river, "is that I have transportation awaiting to cross me back over to the other side of the Chesapeake, for I traveled to Annapolis by buggy, then here by boat. And there is room enough on the cutter for all of us."

"What's the bad news?" Sera asked, a hint of worry creeping into her voice, partly because she could hear a woman screaming in the distance, which seemed odd for such a small town. She couldn't help being on edge. Dak had been surprised that Sera had let Riq out of her sight once she'd found him, but he'd been quick to declare that she'd made the right decision. Dak figured that Riq knew what he was doing. Sera herself was less sure.

"The bad news is that we must go by way of Annapolis. But we'll get that far tonight and take the buggy the rest of the way. We'll reach Baltimore in the morning."

"That's not so bad," Sera said.

"There's even worse news, though," Dak said, turning and glancing over his shoulder. "I just saw our non-Friend, Mrs. Beeson, in front of the hotel, and I'm guessing she saw us, too, because now we're being followed. Gammy, do you know those two guys?"

Gamaliel looked over his shoulder, and then began to walk faster. "Not by name," he said in a grim voice. "Time Wardens working as slave traders. They're not fond of me, or my newspaper. I thought I'd managed to lose them on this trip." He waved to catch the attention of someone by the river.

The three hurried to the wharf, Gamaliel directing Dak and Sera to a pilot cutter. "No time to waste now," Gamaliel said under his breath. He held out his hand to Sera, who didn't really need help climbing aboard but thought it would be impolite to say so, and then Dak, who ignored the hand and jumped in on his own. They were getting to be decent sailors themselves by now.

Gamaliel climbed aboard after them. "Go below and stay out of sight," he said to Dak and Sera. "I think we lost them, but best we take precautions." He strode across the deck to speak to the captain.

From their hiding place in the little cabin that led below, Dak and Sera could hear various scuffles and shouting from around the wharf, which seemed to be quite natural as far as wharves go at night, but they still strained to scan the area for the Time Wardens. It was too dark to see much. The only lights were those of oil lamps on the boats and the stars above.

"I wish it was light out," Dak said. He watched the sailors go to work and started explaining to Sera everything he knew about piloting vessels and how their job was to help guide the bigger ships into port. A pilot cutter was kind of like a tugboat, but about a trillion times cooler because it had a mast and could go superfast. Sera nodded now and then, not all that interested. She got up and stood in the doorway of the little cabin as the cutter headed down the river toward the Chesapeake Bay.

"There it is," she said. "The Big Dipper, pointing out the North Star. We're following it. Well, sort of, now that we're turning north." She felt the sharp cut of the wind whipping around her bonnet and slapping her in the face with spray. A Remnant blew through her as well, making her long for her parents. It was crazy, really. She didn't remember them at all, yet she felt such love for them, such intense desire to be with them as if she knew them well.

"I bet you miss your parents," she said to Dak.

He got up and stood behind her, looking out over her shoulder. "Yeah, I do. A lot. I know I make a lot of stupid jokes, but the truth is, I can't stop worrying about them." He took a deep breath and blew it out. "I've been on this very same body of water before with them," he said. "We stayed here on vacation once when we went to Washington, DC, to see the War of 1812 Memorial. We went sailing. It was the best time—" He stopped abruptly and didn't continue. He slipped his hand into his pocket and fingered the iron key his mother had slipped to him when he'd seen his parents for a moment in 911.

Sera grimaced. "We'll see them again. We'll figure it out. We have to."

"At least they're alive."

Sera put on a brave smile. "Right. Exactly. At least you know that much." She swallowed hard and told herself her watery eyes were from the wind.

"I sure hope Riq's okay," Dak said. "He's not going to be safe anywhere during this entire Break. At least when I was on the Viking ship I didn't look like a slave." He drew the heel of his boot along the crack in the planked flooring. "This whole time period really stinks, you know? I just never thought about it like this before. I wish we could fix it all." He held up his hand before Sera could butt in. "I know, I know. We can't. We can only, you know, remove the boulder in the river so the stream flows the way it's supposed to. Or whatever mumbo jumbo poetry you turned the explanation into the other day."

"For the love of mincemeat," Sera muttered. "You know how to ruin a moment, don't you?" She ventured out of the cabin and peered around at the sailors working all around. "I think it's probably safe to wander," she said. "Nobody's going to stow away now."

Just then, a beeping sound came from one of Dak's pockets.

"Is that the SQuare?" asked Sera.

"Um . . . ," said Dak. He dug around in his coat until he finally produced a small electronic device. "I guess my battery is dying."

Sera couldn't believe her eyes. "You've had your cell phone with you this entire time?" she hissed.

Dak looked bashful. "I thought it might come in handy eventually. Like, what if my parents tried to call? But so far we haven't been anywhere with reception."

"Gee, I can't believe you couldn't get a signal in 885 when you'd been abducted by Vikings. That would have been handy." She took the phone from him. "Although, I might be able to use it for spare parts."

"Don't you dare!" Dak said.

They heard footsteps and looked up to see Gamaliel approaching. Sera shoved the phone in her pocket. "How are you two?" he asked. "I wish I could show you the beautiful forest landscape here, but alas, it's all covered by darkness." He smiled. "I know you're worried, but take heart. Annapolis isn't far. Captain Grunder said we're making excellent time. The wind is with us."

"And so are we," came a menacing voice from behind them. Gamaliel and the kids whirled around. The faces of the two Time Wardens loomed out of the darkness. "It seems you have a debt to pay. Our friend Mary sold a slave this morning. Either pay the money or produce the slave. Now." The man sneered. "Or you might not live to see the future again, time travelers."

Lost and Alone

EVERYTHING FELT like a nightmare in slow motion. Riq saw it all, from John slipping and crashing into the oyster boat and unable to move, to Kessiah, holding the baby and helpless to act, to the boat's captain, not willing or able to risk jail and a huge fine for helping a fugitive. Riq rushed to the edge of the water to see if he could toss the boy safely into the boat, but the wind caught the sail, pulling it away quickly, and there was no one on board who could catch him. He couldn't risk it—what if he missed and James plunged into the dark sea? Riq could only hold the little boy tightly and turn to face the threat of three slave traders rushing at him at once.

"Stop right there," Riq growled, trying to sound tough. "I'm here with a whole squad of Hystorians. We know what you SQ are up to."

The men looked puzzled. "What's an SQ?" one said. "Did he just call us a curse word?"

Riq didn't know whether he should be relieved or

disappointed. He'd thought he was up against three sinister SQ agents. But they were only a bunch of jerks.

He yelled out to Kessiah, "We'll meet you there!" He hoped fiercely that she heard him—and trusted him. If she risked coming back, she might be captured for good.

He zigzagged around the oyster piles and began doing soccer drills, stopping and turning just when the men thought they knew where he would be next. Ultimately, he decided his best option would be to head back into the woods, which he did.

It was definitely harder to run with the extra forty pounds on his back after very little food and water all day, but the running helped poor little James forget about the traumatic scene he'd just witnessed. With the promise that he'd see his parents again soon, he began enjoying himself, laughing whenever Riq changed directions. "You're my horse!" he cried, and Riq was actually sad he had to shush the boy.

As he headed into the woods he went on his now familiar route, but when he caught a glimpse of the sky, he remembered the clue. With the men following him closely, he plunged farther into the dark woods, following the Drinking Gourd, in hopes he would eventually reach another port. The three money-hungry slave handlers stayed on his trail, wanting their cut of the sale that never went through. They may not have been with the SQ, but they were villains all the same.

∞

After an hour, Riq was near exhaustion, James was tired of being jostled, and the slave handlers had fallen far behind. Riq's energy petered out, and then, to his chagrin, so did the land. He came to a point of land that was like the top of a rounded triangle, surrounded by water on two sides with the threat of slave catchers on the third. He could go no farther north. As the moon rose, and with the clearing over the water, he could finally see that he was stranded, stuck on the wrong side of the Choptank River where it led into the Chesapeake Bay. His only options were to turn back into the arms of the slavers or to try to hitch a ride from a passing boat, not knowing who, if anyone, out there could be trusted.

Maybe it was because someone else's life depended on him, and maybe because the horrors of the day had finally caught up with him, and maybe it was the constant ache in his head—all the running wasn't helping his broken nose feel better—but for the first time ever, Riq felt like being a Hystorian was truly going to be the end of him.

"I want to get down. Where's my mama?" James asked.

"We're going to meet her in Baltimore."

"Where's Balto-more?"

Riq looked out over the water. "Oh, it's just on the other side of the water, up that way a bit," he said. He smiled, trying to reassure the boy. "We're just going to rest here for a little while."

He could see boats going by now and then: steamboats,

canoes of various sizes—some even with sails—tugboats, and oyster boats like the one Kessiah and John were in. He strained his eyes on the off chance that they were there, looking for them, but he knew better. It was a huge river, and they'd be long gone by now. Riq doubted he and James had traveled more than a few miles, which accounted for a pretty short distance of the coastline.

"Now," he muttered. "Do we hide, or do we try to flag someone down?" He looked around the small clearing on the bank. There was a dead tree and some long grasses that were completely flattened, probably by the nor'easter that came through . . . but it seemed strange that the grass wasn't flat everywhere.

Then Riq heard a sound that emptied his head of all other thoughts. Howling, in the distance. He remembered what Kissy had said about being hunted. About the Bloodhound Law.

Bloodhounds, he thought. *They're using dogs to track us.* And there was no way he could outrun a dog.

He looked around, panicked, worried that the men would come crashing into the clearing, and thinking that if they did, he'd have nowhere to go. He glanced up into the trees, wondering if they could climb one to hide. And then something caught his eye. Something, or someone, was already in the trees.

24

Smooth Sailing

RIQ LOOKED again to make sure he wasn't just seeing a shadow. "Is someone up there?" he called softly. "Stay here," he said to James, setting him on the ground. He ran to the tree and looked up.

There in the branches were two crouched bodies, holding tightly to a small birch-bark canoe. Riq's heart pounded. In the distance a dog howled. "Three slave handlers are chasing us," he whispered to them. "Please . . . can you help us?"

The two young men looked at each other, but they didn't say anything.

"Please," Riq pleaded. "We don't have anywhere else to go. We're trapped. I can give you"—he looked around, realizing that even though he had a little money in his wallet, they might question a five-dollar bill with a picture of George McClellan on it many years before the man became president—"I'll give you my coat," he said. "Please."

The two spoke in soft tones for a moment, and then

one hopped to the ground. The other balanced the canoe on a branch and then slowly pushed it so that it tipped down. The one on the ground reached for the point. Riq helped grab it and bring the canoe safely down. "Thank you," he whispered. The other dropped to the ground, and wordlessly the three carried the canoe to the water.

"Come on, James," Riq said. His lungs swelled with the brisk air and the hope that they weren't doomed after all, and this time James and his blanket made it safely into the canoe. There were no seats, only a few crossbars, so Riq deposited the boy on the floor, then he helped push off from the bank and jumped inside.

Riq climbed to the front of the canoe to sit with James and grabbed a paddle. He was glad he didn't have to steer and just happy to use his arms for once instead of running. The water parted before them. Within minutes the peaceful waves lulled young James to sleep.

When they were out in the open water with no one nearby, Riq shifted, easing his body around to face the others without tipping them, and began rowing backward now. "Thank you," he said quietly to the two, knowing his voice would travel over the water. "I'm Riq, this is James." He set his paddle down and started taking off his coat as promised.

"It's all right. Keep it. You're going to need that," said the young man in the middle. His voice was suspiciously high-pitched.

Riq raised an eyebrow and the young man in the

middle took off his hat, revealing that he was actually a she. "My name is Anna. This is my husband, Ben." She shifted her position. "We left from Norfolk but had to stop and take shelter when the nor'easter hit—it was too much for this little thing. We were stuck up in that tree for two days. Once the weather cleared this morning, we've been waiting for dark. We were just about to set off again when we heard you all crashing through the woods like a herd of cows."

Riq smiled. "I was getting pretty tired by the end. Thank you again for allowing us to join you. I don't know what we would have done. Where are you headed?"

The woman glanced back at her husband and he shrugged. "North," he said. "But the canoe only takes us to the port where the tall houses meet the water. When we get there, we have to leave it at the wharf with a schooner called *Chariot*—the word looks like this." Ben put his paddle down and pulled something from his pocket. He held out a wrinkled piece of paper with the word spelled out. "The captain will deliver the canoe back to Norfolk for the next folks. He's a good man."

"Clearly," Riq said, awe in his voice.

"Our friends turned back because of the storm or there'd be no room for you," Anna said.

Riq nodded. "I'm feeling very lucky right about now," he said.

"We're not there yet," Ben said.

They paddled in silence through the night, the moon lighting their way. Once they had the west bank of the

Chesapeake Bay in view, they traveled north, following the star, on the lookout for a large deepwater naval port where the three- and four-story houses sprang up from the water.

As Riq's anxiety quelled and the rhythmic paddling calmed his mind, he looked down at James, who was curled in a ball at his feet. *Poor Kessiah,* he thought. *She must be really upset wondering where her little boy could be.* Riq stopped paddling to shed his coat, tucking it around the sleeping boy's body. It reminded him of something a mom or dad would do—or a grandma, in his case. His parents never seemed to have time to think about Riq much at all.

Absently, Riq ran his hand over the boy's head, feeling the prickle of a recent haircut. James's ear was cold, and Riq adjusted the coat to cover it. He found himself wondering if he'd ever find Kessiah. And if he didn't, or if something unthinkable happened to her . . .

"We'll find your mom," Riq said softly, and then he looked up, embarrassed. But the married couple hadn't heard—they continued rowing tirelessly.

Riq returned his paddle to the water as emotions tugged at him from all directions, threatening to strangle him. Because here he was, a Hystorian above all else, just like his parents. Noble. Brave. Always, *always* fighting and sacrificing to do what was best for the Hystorian quest. It was the only thing Riq knew how to do. It was in his blood! It was his destiny. Yet, right here in front of him, in a little heap at his feet, was one individual, one helpless child, whose life depended on Riq.

Riq didn't know what dangers and challenges awaited him in the hours and days ahead as he worked to fix this Break. But suddenly it felt like it didn't matter as much. Because here was this boy who desperately needed Riq. And on the other side of the water was a mother who was counting on him.

Riq's objective had shifted. And while there was still no doubt he would sacrifice *himself* for the Hystorians, he knew that he would not—could not—sacrifice this boy's safety for the good of the world.

He frowned at the water. Had his parents ever made a choice like this?

∞

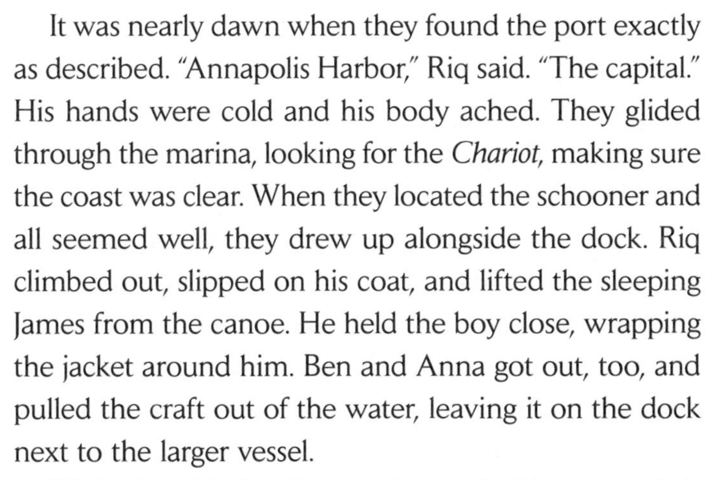

It was nearly dawn when they found the port exactly as described. "Annapolis Harbor," Riq said. "The capital." His hands were cold and his body ached. They glided through the marina, looking for the *Chariot,* making sure the coast was clear. When they located the schooner and all seemed well, they drew up alongside the dock. Riq climbed out, slipped on his coat, and lifted the sleeping James from the canoe. He held the boy close, wrapping the jacket around him. Ben and Anna got out, too, and pulled the craft out of the water, leaving it on the dock next to the larger vessel.

With a handshake all around, they decided to go their

separate ways, knowing that traveling together would only arouse more suspicion. But everyone hoped the cover of a larger city with a larger population of free blacks would allow them to blend in.

As Ben and Anna turned to go, Riq hesitated and then stopped them. "By the way," he said, "there's been some trouble in the safe houses. I was captured from one by someone posing as a Quaker." He looked at the ground, not wanting to give himself away, but wanting to protect his new friends. "If you can avoid the safe houses, you should."

Anna looked grateful. "Thank you," she said.

Ben smiled. "It is a sad thing, not knowing who to trust. But I'm glad we trusted you. You have made our burdens somewhat lighter this night."

"I feel the same way—trust me on that, too." Riq pressed his lips together, gave them a firm nod and a final thank-you, and turned with James to walk along the river, leaving the couple in the shadow of the *Chariot.*

Riq grew fearful that if he didn't get some sleep and some food soon, he might collapse. Had it really been less than twenty-four hours since he ate fish and corn bread at the plantation? He carried the boy along the Severn River, past the Naval shipyard, to a road called King George Street that bridged the river. A sign pointed out the most amazing news of the mission so far for Riq: BALTIMORE, 25 MILES.

"Twenty-five miles," he mused. In the twenty-first century, it would take a half hour. Now? It might take all day if he had to walk. "Not fast enough," he said under his breath. "We need to get there before something happens to your mama."

James was still asleep so he didn't answer.

Riq shivered in the cold and decided the only way to wake up was to keep walking. Nobody was about to offer them a ride. He thought about hiking through the woods, but he'd had enough of that in the dark—his body had been poked and scratched by enough sticks already. His feet were sore and he could feel blisters forming. He wasn't going to go off-road until it was totally necessary. Maybe he wasn't thinking right because of lack of food and sleep, but he was about at the end of his wits. He started to jog and tried to look at the bright side. At least carrying a forty-pound kid around would add some muscle to Riq's body. He should be in pretty great shape by the time they all returned home. . . .

Assuming, of course, he still had a home once they got through this. He cradled James's head on his shoulder and kept jogging toward Baltimore.

∞

They'd gone a short distance when they came upon a stagecoach in front of a building. Riq's curiosity was piqued when he saw the side of the wagon. U.S. MAIL, it said. He stopped, stepping off to the side of the road and into the shadows of the trees, and watched as a man came out rolling a wooden cart that held a stack of crates. He loaded them into the wagon.

When he returned the wooden cart to the building, Riq heard the man shout his thanks to the ones working inside. "Baltimore. Back by noon. Have the next load waiting," he said. He walked back to the stagecoach, and as soon as he was out of sight, Riq made his move. He snuck up to the back of the wagon, set James inside, then, as the horses began to move, he climbed aboard and hid. Within five minutes, he had fallen fast asleep.

25

A Juggling Match

THE TWO men shoved Gamaliel to the ground of the cabin. Dak saw Sera's hand go to her belt to protect the Infinity Ring. They both took a few steps backward, but there was nowhere to go—and the men bearing down on them weren't after Gamaliel, they were after them!

"Time travelers? What are you talking about? And we don't owe you a cent!" Dak said, trying his hardest to sound innocent while staring at what looked to be a saber, circa 1840, the point of which was approximately four inches from his nose. Was it wrong that he wanted to get an even closer look? Because if that was wrong, Dak didn't want to be right.

"Whatcha hiding around your waist, little girl? Hake, grab her and take a look."

"Sure thing, Stuckey."

"Don't touch them," Gamaliel said with a growl.

"Shut him up first," Stuckey said.

Hake followed the order by slamming Gamaliel Bailey up against the wall, shoving a handkerchief in his mouth, and then spinning the man around. He started wrapping a rope around Gamaliel's wrists.

"There sure is a lot of rope around here," Dak muttered. "You could make a whole lotta shoestrings with that. Whole lotta *shoe*strings."

Sera's brows knit together. She glanced down at her feet. "Yes, yes you could. At least one, two, maybe *three*!" she cried. Both Dak and Sera kicked out at once, Dak making contact with Stuckey's hand so that he yanked it up and away and the saber stuck in the ceiling, and Sera aiming high to connect with the man's chest, sending Stuckey reeling into Hake, whose head smashed into the wall. Sera dove between his legs and scrambled out the door while Dak grabbed the saber and pulled it out of the ceiling. He dodged around Stuckey's outstretched leg, and pounded the Time Warden's thigh with the butt of the saber as he went past, hoping to give the man a wicked charley horse.

They dashed out of the cabin and tore through the cutter, startling the ship hands. "There are two men after us! They've got Dr. Bailey held hostage up in the cabin!" Dak shoved the saber at one of the sailors, who took it gratefully and ran to go abaft.

Just then, Stuckey came pounding out of the cabin. Sera shrieked and ran aft, but there was not much she could do other than continue to run around the deck. Dak tried to tackle the Time Warden, but it was like trying to tackle one of the pillars on the White House. He bounced right off and fell to the deck, breathless.

Stuckey chased after Sera, who tripped on the hem of her dress and fell sprawling. "Oof!" she said. She scrambled to her feet again, her knees and palms stinging like crazy, and then before she could pick up speed, Stuckey caught her by the shawl and yanked. The shawl clotheslined Sera and then came off in his hand, exposing the Infinity Ring's satchel around her waist. Stuckey grabbed Sera by the shoulder, whirled her around, and ripped the instrument off her belt.

"You give that back!" Sera screamed in the man's ear as loud as she could, jumping for the Infinity Ring and digging her fingernails into his neck. She wrenched the Ring from him again and punched him in the eye. He staggered back, apparently not knowing quite who he was dealing with.

"Dak! Catch!" Sera shouted and tossed the Ring to him. He caught it and ran the other way.

Stuckey ran around the deck in the opposite direction to face Dak head-on. He charged at the boy, butting into Dak's stomach with his head. Wild-eyed and breathless, Dak threw the Ring back to Sera as he plummeted to the deck with a *thud,* but the toss was too high. Even though she jumped, it sailed over Sera's head and plunked into the dark water off the edge of the boat.

Without a second's hesitation, Sera took a running leap, vaulting over the side, and dove into the icy water after it.

26

Girl Overboard

"MAN OVERBOARD!" yelled one of the sailors at the back of the ship. He immediately dropped the saber Dak had given him and reached for a cylindrical cork life preserver attached to a rope, like an oversized Frisbee. He flung it behind the boat with all his might. Within seconds the word traveled around the ship and the sailors reacted.

"Sera!" Dak screamed. The water was freezing. She could die. He turned to Stuckey and screamed, "I hate you!" And then, spying the saber, he picked it up and ran at the man, brandishing it before him.

"Watch it, kid!" Stuckey yelled, scooting around the blade. "You're the one who threw it in the water. If she drowns, it's on your head, not mine."

The worst thing about that, for Dak, was that it was completely true. With a wild yell he waved the saber, and then drew it back to stab it through Stuckey's heart. Stuckey scrambled out of the way and ran smack into three equally enormous sailors who had come running when the distress call went out. It took them about four seconds to have Stuckey restrained, and then one of them grabbed Dak around the waist and lifted him up. "Let's not have anybody lose any body parts just yet," the sailor said. "We'll focus on your friend first, and we'll deal with him later."

Dak flailed for a minute, and then slowly his senses returned. He handed over the saber with a shuddered breath. "Sera!" he called out. "Sera!" His voice grew ragged from screaming, but he didn't let up.

While the sailor who had thrown the preserver peered out into the darkness and then pulled a small raft from the hold, the rest of the crew had immediately dropped anchor so that the boat could slow to a stop. The sailor carried the raft over the side and dropped it into the water. Deftly, he climbed in and began to paddle. "No sightings yet," he called back to the ship.

"Sera!" Dak screamed into the night. He had already lost his parents. Now his second-worst nightmare was coming true.

∞

Sera's eyes never left the Infinity Ring. She felt the frigid water on her face and hands first, and then, as it seeped through her clothes, she fought the urge to hyperventilate, for the chill nearly shocked her into sucking in a whole lot of water. But as a scientist, she knew how her body would react. As a swimmer, she knew a lot about chasing rings underwater. And as an inventor, there was no way she could let something so life altering go that easily. She figured she had about a half of a second before the Ring sank too far for her to see it in the darkness, and she would risk her life for that half of a second. Without question. Period.

Her eyes stung with cold and salt water as she followed the Ring down. She knew exactly how a figure-eight-shaped object of the Ring's density and weight would react when crashing head-on with seawater that was roughly forty degrees Fahrenheit. And she knew that her own momentum and weight would allow her to travel at a much faster rate through water. So all she had to do was not lose sight of it.

But it was dark down there. A lot went through her mind, the first of which was a mistake so obvious that she wanted to kick herself and no, it wasn't tossing the Infinity Ring on a boat, even though that hadn't been the smartest thing to do. It was this: They'd been in the water with the Ring before. She should have thought to add some sort of phosphorus coating to it after that so it would glow in the dark. She also should have encased it in something that would allow it to float. But can a girl find Styrofoam anywhere in 1492, or 1792, or 885, or even the 1800s? Not a chance.

As it sank just beyond her grasp and the world grew black, she realized the one and only thing Dak's cell phone would be good for at this point. She wriggled her hand into her pocket and pulled it from her sopping-wet dress. *There is, indeed, an app for this,* she thought with tremendous satisfaction. She punched the screen and it began to glow, shining out a good five feet in front of her.

And there it was. The Infinity Ring.

Her lungs burned, and her brain and ears told her to go up, not farther down. But she didn't listen to either one. Instead she held the phone in one hand and propelled herself forward with the other. Nothing else mattered, not the brackish water nor the gross seaweed nor, heaven forbid, an icky fish scooting past. She blocked it all out. Finally, her ears pounding and her lungs screaming inside of her, she reached the Ring. She slipped her bumbling, numb fingers around it, scrambled around in the water, and pushed herself in the opposite direction, toward the moon, hoping to break the surface before she blacked out.

∞

She did. Just when she thought she could bear it no longer, she saw that she was nearly there, which gave her the extra energy to shuttle forward. Her entire body ached with cold so sharp she could hardly stand it. She gasped when she broke through the surface, taking the pressure off her lungs, drawing in precious freezing cold air over and over, and then she flipped to her back, chest heaving. The Quaker clothing was weighing her down—the boots, too, making her feel like her feet were made of cement blocks.

She got her breath back, and then she attempted to look around to see if there was anyone nearby who could help her, or if she'd just freeze to death anyway, after all of that effort. Her mind grew fuzzy with the pain of the cold water wrapped around her. The cell phone, now useless, dark, and waterlogged, drifted from Sera's grasp and sank. She struggled with fiercely shaking fingers to shove her hand through one of the circles of the Infinity Ring as far as she could, trying to get it on her wrist, so that when her dead body washed ashore all puffy and bloated, the Ring would be there for Dak so he could get home.

She turned her head to look around, knowing that if she could keep her wooden legs moving, she could keep floating for a while. She saw the cutter in the distance, and when she raised her head out of the water, she could hear them yelling. "That's good," she told herself through chattering teeth. "That's good. They must know I'm out here." She began to kick in a clumsy manner, as best she could. And then she felt something slither over her neck.

"Gross!" she whispered, sure it was a water snake or an eel or something awful like that. It gave her a burst of adrenaline, but when the snake kept slithering, she reached her numb fingers to get it off of her. With all her effort, Sera lifted it up. It was a rope.

"That's it," said a friendly voice she'd never heard before. "Try to slip your arm through it, Sera. Can you hear me?"

Sera thought he meant the Infinity Ring. She nodded in the water, making a wave splash up in her nose. "I did already," she whispered, bumping her numb hand against the Ring. She could feel herself sinking and she struggled to stay up, but wave after wave washed over her face.

"Sera!" The voice was sharper now. "Put your arm through the life preserver. Do it!"

Sera shuddered and opened her eyes. She saw the life preserver wavering at the edge of her vision, and she heaved her dead-feeling arm into it.

"That's it," said the voice. "I'm almost there. Hang on; I'm going to pull you. Whatever you do, don't let go. Okay?"

"Okay," Sera whispered. She felt her body move through the water, and soon, the hands belonging to the voice were reaching down, pulling her from under her arms, and dragging her out of the cold ocean into the even colder air. But at least she could breathe.

"Stay with me, now," the voice said.

∞

Dak had killed his best friend. It wasn't all-out murder; it was more like reckless endangerment leading to manslaughter or something. Second degree, maybe third or fourth . . . he wasn't very up on his legal terminology, he realized. He buried his face in his hands, feeling utterly miserable and helpless. He sank to the deck and curled up, hugging his knees and resting his forehead on them. His life was over.

He didn't even care about the stupid Infinity Ring. He didn't care that he was stuck here . . . he and his *(cough)* favorite person in the world, Riq, who by virtue of his skin color in this part of the world was considered to be chattel. What a life they'd have. "We'd obviously move to Canada," he muttered. Or London, or some other cool place where people were treated better. But once they did that, Dak didn't really care what happened. Nothing mattered without Sera. She was the only one who really understood him, and he had caused her demise.

Every second that ticked by, every minute, made the truth inevitable. The sailors scurried around him, but Dak paid no attention to them. All he knew was that he had a useless SQuare in his pocket, and he may as well hand it over to the SQ's Time Wardens. The one person responsible for finally figuring out how to finish a time-travel device had now taken all her secrets with her to her watery grave.

"Reel 'em in!" shouted a sailor. "He's got her in the boat. Go, go, go!"

Dak raised his head. "H-he's got her?"

The sailor looked over. "Yes." He didn't sound very excited.

"Is she . . . ?" He couldn't say it.

"I don't know, son." He hopped over the rail and hooked himself to the boat with a lanyard harness. He reached down. "Look smart now," he said to another sailor as they hauled Sera up over the railing, her eyes closed and water thundering to the deck from every part of her, and laid her down.

The Wee Hours

SERA OPENED her eyes to find Dak hovering over her. She had never been so cold in her entire life and she couldn't stop shaking. "Hey, mouth breather, will you get out of my face, please? When's the last time you brushed your teeth? Your breath smells like Vígi's."

Dak looked up at the sailors and Captain Grunder, who looked on, silent. "Yep, she's normal," he said. The crew gave a round of applause as Sera sat up, then shakily got to her feet. Someone shoved a blanket at her, and Dak wrapped it around her and held on to her arm so she didn't fall.

"Back at it, men!" the captain shouted. He looked at Sera. "We don't, er, have any spare getups for thee." He blushed. "But I can give thee something to wear until thy clothes are dry."

"Anything will be fine as long as it's not a dress," Sera said, teeth chattering loudly.

"Aye, it is no dress." He handed a stack of clothes to her. "Make thy way to the cabin for some privacy—the crew is removing the stowaways and tending to Dr. Bailey now. They're stuffing the wood stove full for thee." The kindhearted captain blushed again and departed. "We'll be at the harbor in no time."

Sera grabbed on to Dak and they hurried to the cabin, walking by two sailors with Hake. Sera glared at him as she passed. Gamaliel was just easing his way out of the cabin, a bandage on his head but otherwise looking as healthy as ever.

"Sera!" he exclaimed. "I'm so relieved to see you're all right, and so sorry I wasn't of more help. I feel terrible about that."

"Don't worry. Everything's fine."

"And the . . . the device?"

Sera pulled her sleeve up and showed him. "Hopefully I can get it back off my wrist again."

Dak let out a sigh of relief. He hadn't dared to ask.

Gamaliel and Dak stepped out of the cabin so Sera could change. She stuck her boots by the stove, put on the captain's breeches and shirt, fairly swimming in them, and rolled over the waistband, tying a rope around the waist to keep the pants up. Then she added thick, itchy wool socks and put her dry shawl back on over her shirt. She huddled by the stove. "You can come back in now," she called. Carefully, she worked the Infinity Ring off her wrist and with relief, hid it in the draping shirt.

Dak took one look at her and burst out laughing. "You look funny," he said. "Ow." He grabbed his stomach, sore from where the Time Warden had plowed into him.

"Dak . . ."

"No, wait—oh, my henna, get this." He framed his hands so they made a marquee. "Did you realize you're wearing—drumroll please—Captain Grunder's pants! Get it? That one book from third grade? Captain Grunderpants? Remember?"

Sera glared at him. "No."

"It was about those two guys who make a superhero—"

"For the love of mincemeat, how close to drowning does a girl have to come to get some peace?" Sera said.

Dak snorted and tried very hard to be quiet. It didn't last long.

"I'm sorry," he said, choking back a laugh. "Captain Grunder. His pants. Oh, man." He had to leave the room. Very, very suddenly.

Sera stared at the source of heat. Her teeth still chattered, and she knew they probably would for a while, but that was a good thing. It would be a bad sign if she got so cold her teeth stopped chattering. So she knew she'd be fine. But almost losing the Infinity Ring really made her think about things. Maybe she could shackle it to herself. No, that wasn't even a little bit funny to imagine after the shackles she'd seen lately. She'd just have to keep using the satchel—sopping wet though it was.

∞

A few minutes later, there was a knock at the door.

"Are you finally done laughing?" Sera called out.

The door pushed open. It was the sailor from the raft—the one who had saved her. His dark brown eyes shone when he saw her sitting up, the color back in her face—or back out of it, since her lips weren't blue anymore. He stood for a moment, his hat in his hand. He pulled something from his pocket. "I brought you this," he said. He held it out to her. "I found it on the deck. I'm sorry it's broken."

It was the gold chain that Bill had given her back in the year 911. She gasped. "I didn't even realize I'd lost it!" she said. She stood up and threw her arms around his waist, hugging him. "Thank you! It's very valuable—very meaningful—to me." She looked up at his face, his deep brown skin several shades darker than her own. "Thank you for saving me," she said, feeling a little bit shy.

"You're welcome," he said. "That's my job. And now that we're heading into the Annapolis Harbor, I'd better get back out there before the captain tans my hide." He smiled.

Sera frowned. "Would he do that?"

The man tilted his head and smiled. "No, miss—it was just an expression."

"Forgive my asking, but are you—are you all free?" Sera asked, hoping it was not impolite, but she was suddenly very curious what kind of man's pants she was wearing—and if they were those of a slave owner.

"We're all free, yes, miss. Got our papers to prove it." He reached for his pocket.

"Oh! No—no need for that." She waved off his efforts. "I was just wondering what kind of man Captain Grunder is."

The sailor smiled and reached for the door. "He's one of the good ones." With a wink, he swung open the door and went back out.

"And so are you, sir," Sera said to the closed door, holding up a chain of gold that last week had been new, but today was nearly a thousand years old.

28

Good Morning, Baltimore!

LUCKILY, JAMES woke up when the U.S. Mail stagecoach stopped. He shook Riq awake. "I'm so hungry," the boy whined, gripping his stomach.

Riq, forgetting not only where he was but also what year he was in, took a moment to get his bearings. Then he realized they weren't moving. He sat up and shook his fuzzy brain. "Okay, buddy," he said. "*Shh,* now. I'll find you something to eat. But we've got to be quiet."

"I don't want to be quiet. Where's my mama?"

"We're going to see her right now." Riq peered out the back of the wagon and then hopped out. "Come on," he whispered.

James stopped fussing and climbed out, jumping to the ground.

"Follow me," Riq said. He snuck around to the road's edge and began walking uphill like he had a purpose, even though he'd completely lost his bearings.

A stray chicken clucked at him from the side of

the road. Riq glanced around, and then lunged at it. It jumped and skittered around him. Riq tried again, this time managing to scoop it up so it would look like he was delivering something. The chicken flapped and squawked, and Riq almost dropped it, but then it settled down. Riq carried it like a football. His heart pounded. There were white people and black people moving about in buggies and on foot. "Are you still behind me?" he said once, his eyes never leaving the road, constantly scanning the area for anyone who looked like they'd be dangerous or threatening.

"Yes, sir," James said. He kicked a stone, and it hit Riq in the leg.

"Good job," Riq said. "You're doing great, buddy. Don't kick any more stones, though. Please." He wished the chicken would lay an egg so he could eat it. His stomach twisted with hunger.

When they reached a cross street, Riq saw a black boy about his age. "Where's Federal Hill?" he asked in a low voice.

The boy looked at Riq. "You're standing on it," he said.

"And the lookout spot is . . . ?"

The boy pointed up to the top of the hill.

Riq scanned the horizon and saw his destination. His heart surged. "Here, have a chicken," he said, handing the animal to the startled boy. And then he reached his hand back and looked down at his traveling companion. He smiled. "Come on, James. Let's go find your mama."

James grabbed Riq's hand and together they ran the

hundred yards up the hill as fast as they could go. As they approached the observatory, young James broke from Riq's grasp and sprinted ahead.

∞

If there had been a war, Gamaliel Bailey, Dak, and Sera would have fit right in with those who returned injured. Gamaliel with his bandaged head sat beside the two kids, one who was dressed like a sailor but carried dripping Quaker woman's garb, and the other who was curled up after being socked in the gut by a thug. They were a sight to behold.

After they'd said their good-byes to the crew of the cutter, Gamaliel had guided them to the stables where his horse and buggy waited. They had all climbed in and with a soft-spoken command they were off at a brisk pace to Baltimore.

After a time, Gamaliel nudged Dak. "We're nearly there," he said. As the buggy began its journey up the hill, the weak December sun shone through the clouds, and the air was not quite as brisk as it had been. Sera stretched and rerolled her pant legs, tucking them inside her boots so she didn't trip once they were ready to get out of the buggy. She pulled the shawl close around her shoulders, knowing she looked like a total weirdo, but she didn't care. In fact, nothing that had happened to her was on her mind now. She was focused on Riq, hoping nothing bad had happened to him. It would be so typical for something else to go wrong right about now.

Gamaliel stopped the buggy and the three climbed out. Gamaliel tied the reins to the hitching post. Sera looked at Dak, Dak looked at Sera, and both of them crossed their fingers. Leaving Gammy behind, they ran the rest of the way up the hill to the observatory, dread twisting in the pit of Sera's stomach at every step.

When they neared the meeting spot, Sera squealed. "Riq!" She tore ahead of Dak and tackled her friend, knocking him to the ground.

"Watch the nose!" he said. He took one look at her and started laughing. "I don't even want to know what happened to you," he said. When Dak joined the party on the hill, Riq gave them both a smile—one of the most genuine smiles they had ever seen on him. He reached out and slung his arms around their shoulders. "You have no idea how happy I am to see you guys," he said. But his smile quickly faded. "Now we just need to find Kissy and John."

29

The Job Has Just Begun

STANDING TOGETHER on Federal Hill, Sera introduced Gamaliel to Riq, but Riq could barely concentrate enough to shake hands with the man. *Where are they?* he wondered.

He trained his eyes on the bay below, straining to see any sign of Kissy or John. Absently, he recounted to the others what had happened to him and how he came to be traveling with James.

Meanwhile, Gamaliel went in search of breakfast for everyone. After the man returned with food, he stationed himself as a guard, keeping an eye out for SQ and slave traders. After a time, he spoke. "Perhaps we should find a safer place to wait."

Riq frowned, scanning the area as people walked here and there. He knew the Hystorian was right—he and James weren't safe out in the open like this. But he couldn't go back on his last words to Kissy. He couldn't risk them missing each other. "No," he said, determined.

"I promised her we'd be here. We can't leave. There's no way she won't be here."

On the inside, Riq's confidence crumbled. He could think of two things that could stop her. He looked at James, who'd been collecting sticks and brown crunchy leaves and rotting acorn caps. The boy squatted in the dirt, making a fort out of his supplies. Riq leaned over and wiped a smudge of dirt from James's face. *What have I done?*

Dak sat down to play with the boy while Sera joined Riq on the lookout for the missing parents. Riq couldn't stand still. What if something had happened to Kissy and John? What on earth was Riq supposed to do with James if they didn't show up?

Riq felt Sera's hand on his arm. He stopped pacing.

"I'm *sure* they're coming," she said.

Riq shook his head and looked at her, his nose throbbing, his body exhausted. "I'm just . . . I'm afraid I made a really big mistake. And I'm not sure . . . what . . . to do. . . ." He swallowed hard and massaged his temples, trying to hide his pooling eyes. "I shouldn't have insisted on going with them. If I'd just stayed with you guys and the Hystorian . . ."

"Then James would have been left alone on shore and captured by those slave traders, and he'd *never* see his parents again." Sera folded her arms. "Is that what you want? You'd rather just not have to deal with him? Because the Hystorian quest is so much more important?" Her eyes flared.

"No!" Riq felt heat rising to his face. "That's not it at all. I'm just not sure what we're supposed to do now. I messed everything up."

"Well," Sera said, "it seems to me you did something right. And I'm not worried." Her voice grew thick. "Parents have a way of finding their children. Even when it seems impossible. I'm just sure of it." She turned away and blinked rapidly.

Riq was quiet. He thought of Dak's parents whizzing through time, shoving the key into Dak's hand before they disappeared, trying their best to help their son even when they needed help themselves. And he thought of Sera, whose Remnants had her convinced of the bond she shared with a mother and father she never knew. And then he thought of his parents. After a moment he scraped the ground with his shoe. "Yeah," he said. "Maybe."

"She'll be here," Sera said again. "If she doesn't come, then there's no hope for any of us."

You don't know how right you are, Riq thought.

∞

A short while later, a timid-looking woman with dark brown skin approached. She looked at James, and then turned to Riq.

"May we help you?" Riq asked. He felt a surge of hope—maybe this woman knew where Kissy was.

"I'm looking for Riq."

"That's me."

She pointed at the boy. "That James?"

"Maybe. Why?"

"Kessiah sent me to give you a message," the woman said.

Riq's eyes widened. "What is it?"

"I'm to tell you she's found Aunt Harriet and wishes you to meet her in Wilmington. She has sent a wagon to collect you." The woman looked up. "Come with me. I'll take you there."

"Is she okay?" Sera asked. "Is everything all right?"

"She's fine," the woman said. "She said not to worry. Just come."

"Where in Wilmington?" Dak asked, eyes narrowed.

The woman rattled off the response as if she'd been expecting the question. "The home of Aunt Harriet's Quaker friend, Thomas Garrett."

Gamaliel harrumphed, catching Riq's attention. The man's brow was furrowed and he shifted uneasily. Riq caught his eye and the two exchanged a look before Riq turned back to the woman.

"*Kessiah* said that?"

"Yes."

"And she's with *Aunt Harriet*?"

"Yes," she said with a huff. "Now, if you'll please follow me."

"It will be our pleasure," said Gamaliel.

The woman shook her head. "Just the two, James

and Riq—they're all I'm supposed to collect," she said, looking at the Latina and the Caucasian of the group, and eyeing Gamaliel suspiciously.

"Oh," Dak said. "We're all family. Aunt Harriet won't mind."

The woman looked confused, but said nothing. "I'm not sure they're expecting so many . . . for dinner."

"We don't eat much," Sera said.

The woman knew when she was beat. She turned to walk down the hill, glancing behind her to check that the group was following.

Riq had an idea. He let Gamaliel round up James and walk ahead with the woman, while he fell back into step with Dak and Sera. In a low voice, he began speaking in Tlingit. Immediately, Dak and Sera's earpieces, which they hadn't used at all in this era, clicked in to the language and translated.

"Something isn't right, you two. Kissy calls her aunt *Minty,* not *Harriet.* And I don't believe for a second that she'd go on ahead to Wilmington without James."

"You think she's in trouble?" asked Dak. His translator tooth cap did its job translating the words to Tlingit.

Riq nodded. "Someone must have captured Kissy and John, and discovered they were headed here. Now they're after James and me, so they can sell us all over again."

"Too bad they didn't count on us," Sera said.

"Exactly," Riq said. "I say we pretend like we buy her story, and when we get there, we'll barge in and throw a wrench in their operation. With any luck, we'll catch an SQ agent and be able to learn something about their larger plan. It can be our first step in getting the Underground Railroad back on its tracks before it derails for good."

"Great plan," Sera said.

"Agreed," said Dak.

The three shared a grin. It was good to be back together at last.

30

Onward and Upward

THE TRIP to Wilmington would take most of the day. On the way, James took an immediate liking to their escort and began talking to her nonstop, now that he was finally allowed to talk as much and as loudly as he wanted. Meanwhile, Sera, Dak, and Riq found a spot in the wagon as far away as possible and they continued their quiet conversation in Tlingit.

"I spoke with Gammy. He says Thomas Garrett really does live in Wilmington. He's legit," Sera reported.

"Does he know what Mr. Garrett looks like?" Dak asked.

"Totally."

"Rock on. So we'll know right away if we're dealing with a phony. I'd sure hate to tackle the wrong guy."

"Well, the real Mr. Garrett sounds amazing!" Sera said with a wide grin. "He has this huge house and he gets into trouble all the time for hiding slaves there. In court, he said something like 'you can put me in jail and take all my money, but I'm still going to keep helping people who need help.' He's had to pay a pantsload of fines and he just keeps going! Or at least he did," Sera said, and she turned serious again. "He's one of the Hystorians that nobody's heard from in days."

"That is so not cool," said Riq.

"But you know what definitely is cool?" Sera asked. "It's so amazing that you found your family, Riq, and got to spend some time with them." She looked at her hands. "I guess I'm a little jealous."

Riq flashed a small smile and let out a sigh. "Don't be." He felt a pain in his heart, and for the briefest of moments, he longed to share his personal fears with the other two. But he couldn't, and soon the moment passed, which was for the best. He didn't want anyone trying to talk him out of doing the right thing.

Not feeling like talking much anymore, he lay down on his side and closed his eyes. "We should all get some sleep while we have the chance."

∞

When they arrived, it was early evening. The time travelers got out of the wagon, and James jumped and ran around outside in the open air, entirely fed up with being forced into so many tight places for the past two days. Riq marveled at the boy's energy.

Finally, they all approached the stately home of Thomas Garrett. When they knocked on the door, they were met by a tall, pale woman. Her hair was flaming red, and her lips the color of an oil slick.

Riq sucked in a breath.

"Welcome," she said, sounding totally unwelcoming. "I am Ilsa." Her voice was colder than the Chesapeake Bay.

As she ushered them inside and dismissed the woman who'd led them from Federal Hill, Riq spoke under his breath to Sera and Dak. And since all the Tlingit tongue clicking was getting old, this time he spoke in Russian. "She's the spitting image of Tilda—the Lady in Red."

"The one who wants to take over the SQ?" Sera said. "But how'd she get here without a—"

"Shh," Riq said. "I don't think it *is* her. She just looks like her."

"Is it too late to change our minds about this?" Dak whispered.

The red-haired woman folded her arms and leaned toward the three. "Yes," she said in perfect Russian. "As a matter of fact, it *is* too late." She switched back to English. "Gentlemen," she called out.

Riq heard the door close behind him.

"Yes, ma'am," rang out a choir of voices.

"It appears your hunches were correct." She looked at Gamaliel. "And you've also managed to bring me the next Hystorian on my list. How convenient."

Slowly, they all turned around to find Hake, Stuckey, and several other SQ agents circling them like a pack of starving wolves.

A Trap Is a Trap Is a Trap

DAK PRIDED himself on being smart. But it sure didn't seem as if being smart was enough to keep him from walking into traps every other day.

He'd assumed they'd be up against a single undercover SQ agent, like the fake Mrs. Beeson. He'd assumed they'd have the advantage and that surprise would be on their side. He'd assumed wrong.

But he was smart enough to know when they were beat. As much as he wanted to fight, they didn't have a chance.

Ilsa knew it, too. She smiled an evil smile. "Hake, Stuckey, take the darling Bowley boy to the cellar to wait with the other auction items," she said, voice dripping with contempt. She held up a finger and tapped it to her black lips. "On second thought, let's not give them the satisfaction of seeing the boy. Instead, take them all to the holding room, while I alert my colleagues to the good news of the time travelers' arrival. Most of them have begun their journey here already, so it won't be long. Then we'll have tea and learn about all their little secrets." She laughed a sinister laugh.

James looked scared. Dak tried to reassure him with a strained smile and a wink. "Just stick close to us, buddy," he whispered.

"How are you jerks even here?" Sera asked as Hake grabbed her by the arms. "You attacked us in public! You should be in jail."

Ilsa clucked her tongue. "They were acting within the law in their pursuit of stolen property. Under the Fugitive Slave Act, it's all of you who are the criminals."

Stuckey took the satchel from Sera's belt while Dak dropped his eyes to the ground. "Man, I really hate this time period," he mumbled.

∞

As one of the burly agents rough-armed him down the hallway, Riq glanced around, taking in whatever he could. The house was large, but there was hardly any furniture, which made all the rooms they passed look the same. Soon they reached a locked door. Riq could hear muffled sounds coming from the other side of it. One of Ilsa's cronies pulled his set of keys from his belt and unlocked the door, and Riq and the others were dragged inside.

What they saw shocked them. All along the walls of the unfurnished sitting room stood more than a dozen men and women. There were Quakers next to collared priests, Nanticoke Indians next to Pennsylvania Dutch. Their skin colors ranged from darkest dark to palest pale—it was a true American melting pot. Riq might have choked up at the sight of it, if it weren't for one little thing: Each person in the room was shackled to the wall and gagged.

Riq felt his eyes grow wide as he looked at all the faces in the room, and wider still when the Time Wardens pulled more shackles and gags from a tiny closet.

"Come now," said Gamaliel. "Is it necessary to shackle the children?"

Stuckey rubbed his chest where Sera had kicked him only a day before. "It's necessary. But it's also a pleasure."

There was nothing they could do. Riq watched as his friends were shackled to a bar that ran the length of the far wall. He was the last to be tied down. He hadn't missed the feeling of chains around his wrists. And the gag made it that much worse.

The Time Wardens checked the shackles to make sure they were secure, and then they stalked back out of the room, closing the door behind them.

Dak made a number of muffled noises as he appeared to recognize a few people, trying to shout out their names, but everything he said sounded like "Woowoo woo! Hawweewa eehee oo!"

Riq felt powerless. He couldn't even console James, who was sniffling, trying to dry the tears from his eyes with his shoulder.

It was then that he realized he had completely failed to accomplish his one goal: keeping Kissy and her aunt Minty safe so they didn't get sold back into slavery. How could he have let go of the mission? He'd been arrogant again, and now look at them: Kessiah and John were in a cellar somewhere about to be auctioned off, and Aunt Minty . . . well, he supposed she was in this room somewhere.

He looked around at all the faces, and he was surprised that no one looked scared. They all wore expressions of extreme dignity. These were men and women who didn't break under pressure. They didn't give up when things got tough. They probably didn't even *complain* when things got tough.

Riq felt pride building up inside of him. He thought of all the people throughout history—Hystorians, but other people, too—who had sacrificed everything to help others. The presence of so many heroes in one room gave him the motivation to keep going. He just *had* to get out of here—for James's sake if for no other reason.

There were two African-American women in the room, one who was rather tall and grand looking, and another as short as Sera and somewhat plain. Riq thought back to the pictures from Grandma Phoebe's album and knew by sight that the shorter woman was Aunt Minty—Araminta Harriet Ross Tubman—who he just knew was destined for greatness if it weren't for the SQ. He caught the woman's eye and she managed to make hers twinkle at him. He looked down at the floor, feeling awkward, and when he glanced at her again, she appeared to be asleep on her feet. Perhaps he'd imagined the twinkle.

∞

While Riq was lost in thought and Dak was talking to himself in his newly created fourth language (English, pig latin, Spanish [one word], and now Mufflygag), Sera was kicking herself for not insisting they come up with a better plan before waltzing into an SQ stronghold. What were they going to do now, without anyone to help them? Without a key to unlock these shackles?

Wait a second, she thought. She looked up. "Ah hee!" she cried, though no one could understand her through the gag. Wildly, she kicked Dak. "Ah hee!" she said. "Ah hee!"

"Wha?" Dak scrunched up his face, trying to understand her. "Ahi?"

Sera shook her head violently. "Hee! HAY-HEE-WHY. Hee."

Dak shook his puzzled face. "Wha?" he asked again.

"Ah hee frohm you pahents!"

Riq lifted his head, suddenly alert. He nodded at Sera and tried a different tactic. "Ih you pockeh!"

Dak tilted his head. "Oooh," he said. "Ah *hee.*" He nodded thoughtfully. And then he looked down at his pocket . . . which was nowhere within reach of his shackled hands.

Sera soon realized the problem as well. Her shoulders slumped. *There's no way it could be the right key anyway,* she thought. *What are the odds?* But like she'd said earlier, parents seemed to have a way of finding their children.

And Dak's parents had always been there for him. Always.

A clanging noise from between her and Dak startled her. She looked down at James, and then up at the now empty shackle that had once held his right arm. He shook his wrist, pulled the gag out of his mouth, and grinned. "I did it," James said. He examined his freed wrist and frowned. "Got a scrape."

"Oh!" Sera said. "Me, hoo?" She bent as close to James as she could and tried to say, "Can you take my gag out, too, please?"

James seemed to have no trouble understanding her, and he stretched toward her as far as he could, just barely able to grasp Sera's gag while his left arm remained shackled overhead. He pulled her gag down, and Sera let out a relieved sigh. "Thank you," she said in a whisper. "We still need to be quiet, okay?"

James nodded.

"How did you do that?"

"I made a stick with my hand and pulled it out," James said, matter-of-factly. "This one is still stuck, though." He tugged on the chain to prove it.

Sera smiled at him, then caught Dak's eye. "Can you reach Dak's gag?" she asked.

Dak leaned toward James, and James lunged for the gag, straining against his shackle. "Nope," James said. And then he looked at Sera. "I can reach his pocket, though. Do you want me to get the key you were talking about?"

A burst of muffled chuckling rippled through the room, and Sera realized all the other prisoners had been watching intently. She grinned at the boy. "Yes, please."

Now that he had an audience, James beamed. He strained away from Sera and fished the key from Dak's pocket. Then he twirled around on his chain and strained the other way, trying to get more laughs. He held the key out to Sera, not quite able to reach her hand.

And so he tossed it.

Sera's grin turned to a gasp as the key bounced off her hand and clinked to the ground.

Free at Last?

JAMES COULDN'T reach the floor. He bowed his head in shame. "It's okay," Sera said. She closed her eyes and tried to use her shoulder to wipe the sweat from her forehead. When she opened her eyes again, she realized that everyone in the room had frozen at the sound of the key hitting the floor. Now they watched her, encouragement and praise beaming from the crinkles around their glistening eyes. Sera glanced at Gamaliel, Dak, and Riq, who were all nodding their encouragement. She looked at James, whose bottom lip was trembling. "No worries, kid," she said. "We can do this."

She placed her foot on the key and slid it to the wall. With that done, she took a deep breath and relaxed her muscles, and then she tensed up again and began the painstaking job of pushing a single key up a wall with her foot.

"Glad I'm wearing Grunder's pants, or this could get awkward," she muttered.

She had to move slowly. When her leg began to wobble and shake, Sera closed her eyes. Sweat dripped down her temples now, her thigh muscles burned, but she held her position, gathering her inner strength. And then she began moving once again, centimeter by centimeter, until finally her thumb and forefinger grasped the key. She exhaled, and a murmur swept through the crowd. *So this what it's like to be on a sports team when you're not the one messing up,* she thought.

But it wasn't over yet.

There was no way to get the key in the lock with a hand that was shackled, so she pulled her chained arm toward her mouth instead and yanked her head and torso toward it, straining her neck so that she could clench the key in her teeth.

With her mouth closed around the key, Sera tilted her head slowly, looking cross-eyed at the end of the key in order to line it up with the shackle's lock. She prayed that her hunch was right, knowing that all her efforts could be for nothing.

The room was so silent she could hear mice skittering in the walls. Sera pushed the key into the lock and slid it as far as she could until it hit metal. She took a few breaths now that it was somewhat set in place, and then slowly she tilted her head the other way, eyes closed, listening, until she heard and felt a *click,* and the shackle opened, falling off her wrist and thudding against the wall.

"Hee hee!" she said, one wrist free. She wiped the sweat from her forehead. She grabbed the key from the dangling shackle, freed her other wrist, and looked around the room and grinned. The prisoners were waving their hands in silent applause, and she held a finger to her lips. She shook out her hands to get the blood flowing again, and then she moved around the room unlocking shackles like it was going out of style.

Dak turned to Gamaliel while Sera made the rounds. "Is everyone here a you-know-what?" he asked.

"Everyone present is a Hystorian in addition to being an abolitionist, yes. There's no need for secrecy."

Dak smirked. "Speaking of secrecy, aren't you guys supposed to be a secret organization? How did the SQ manage to track everyone down?"

The short African-American woman answered as Sera unlocked her shackles. "It was the lanterns," she said. "They figured out what the lanterns meant. We led them straight to us."

Riq stepped forward. "Aunt Minty, is that you?" he asked.

She raised her chin. "Do you have my niece?" she said softly.

"She's here in the cellar with her husband and baby. Your journey to help them to freedom may be delayed, but it is by no means cancelled."

Harriet Tubman smiled. "Your encouraging words will carry me."

Gamaliel Bailey stepped forward alongside a large white-haired man wearing a suit. "Dak, Sera, Riq, this is

Thomas Garrett. It's his house that Ilsa has taken over as the hub for this entire plot."

Thomas Garrett smiled. "At your service," he said. "It is a pleasure to know you, although I would have liked it to be under better circumstances." He roared in laughter and was subsequently shushed by a number of people in the room.

"Thank you for your hospitality," Dak said, rubbing his wrists, a grin playing at the corner of his lips. "You have a lovely home, despite your lack of furniture."

"I apologize—I had to sell it all to pay a rather large fine for helping fugitives," the man said.

"Well, that's pretty cool of you," Dak said. He paused. "Do you by chance know the way out of here?"

Thomas Garrett chuckled. "I believe I do. But we have one small hurdle remaining."

Riq heard the concern in Mr. Garrett's voice. "What is it?" he asked.

The man pointed to the door. "Ilsa has locked us in. And there's no way to unlock that door from this side."

In Which the Hystorians Are Reshackled, Only Not Really

DAK AND Sera looked at each other. "I guess this means we'll have to make them open it, then," Dak said. "Unless you have any non-life-threatening scientifically experimental ways to break this lock."

"Come off it, Smyth," Sera muttered. "It was one time. One time!"

"Eyebrows," Dak reminded her.

"You're kind of obsessed with your eyebrows. It's weird."

"Your face is weird."

"Good grief," Riq said. "Could you do this later, please? We've got stuff to do."

"He's right, knock it off," Dak said.

Sera rolled her eyes. "Whatever," she said, turning her attention back to the group. "Here's the plan. Everybody, go back to your places and put your wrists back into the shackles—but for the love of mincemeat, don't close them—just make it look like you've got them on. Gags loosely in your mouths, too. I know, I know, spit-tacularly gross, but this is what we do for the good of society."

Everyone but Riq and Dak went obediently to his or her place and slipped their gags and shackles on.

"I really, *really* like this group of people," Sera muttered. She looked at James. "If fighting happens, you stay out of the way, okay? Just hide in that corner." She pointed, and then she addressed the group once more. "Good, now Ilsa and her thugs took something of mine—something they won't know how to use. I'm going to pretend to offer her instructions in exchange for your freedom," she said. "Just play along like you're trapped there until I say the secret word, which means scream and attack. Once they're in this room they'll be surrounded, and we can overpower them. *Capice?*"

Riq leaned over and whispered, "What's the secret word?"

"The secret word is . . ." Sera pondered it for a moment.

"Eighteen-abibble," Dak said calmly.

Sera looked at him and grinned. "Oh, yeah. I forgot." She looked at the Hystorians. "Eighteen-abibble. Got it?" They all nodded.

Riq shook his head. "Stupidest secret word ever," he muttered.

"Yeah, well, at least nobody will say it by accident. Let's take our places and get ready for a fight."

Just then, the door burst open. Ilsa marched into the

room, followed by an entire squad of SQ agents, including the fake Mrs. Beeson. All were armed, and all looked extremely dangerous.

And in her hand, Ilsa gripped the Infinity Ring.

34

Eighteen-abibble!

SERA, DAK, and Riq, the only ones not yet in their places, whirled around, and their eyes nearly popped out of their heads at the sight of the small army. "Great Wisconsin cheese hats, it's a war Break after all," Dak said. His lip curled at the sight of fake Mrs. Beeson.

Ilsa looked furious. "You're too sneaky for your own good! But no matter. I don't think you're going anywhere without this." She lifted the Ring into the air.

Sera's heart sank to see the device in enemy hands, but she knew she could still fix this. She didn't dare spring the trap yet, though. The SQ had weapons; the Hystorians had nothing. Not safe at all.

"Get her," the woman said, icy calm.

The Time Wardens grabbed Dak and Riq, and pulled them aside. Sera glanced at Gamaliel and Harriet Tubman and Thomas Garrett, who looked poised to leap to her aid, and shook her head the slightest bit. *No, no, no,* she chanted in her head. She wasn't giving up this easily. *Wait for the signal.*

Then Stuckey grabbed her by the arm and she gave him a weary look. "Not you again. Easy on the duds," she muttered. Stuckey pushed her forward to face the red-haired woman. "You've got me. I'll do whatever you say."

Ilsa narrowed her eyes, regarding Sera for a long, suspicious moment.

"Can you tell dog breath to let go of me, please?" Sera asked.

"Settle down, dog breath," Ilsa muttered, turning the Infinity Ring in her hands with the utmost care. "How does it work?" she demanded.

"Well," Sera said, jabbing her elbow into Stuckey's gut and leaning forward. "You program it to the time and place you want to visit and press GO, and then whenever you're ready to return here just press GO again and it'll bring you home automatically. That feature's kind of like the LAST button on your TV remote." She nodded knowingly. "It's slick."

Ilsa frowned at the strange words. "How do you tell it where to go?" Her tone was still harsh, but curious.

"It's very precise, I'm afraid. I've spent forty years learning how to use it."

"Forty years?" Ilsa spat out. "You're a child."

Sera gave Ilsa a strange look. "I beg your pardon? We all look like this at sixty-five." She laughed. "I mean, I figured you must be at least a hundred and fifty years old, maybe one seventy-five, right?"

Ilsa's face burned.

"No?" Sera's voice faltered. "Oh, my bad. I apologize.

I'm sure you're, um, not bad looking for this day and age. Can I get a woof woof?"

"Just show me how to use it. Now," Ilsa barked.

"I can't do it on command. You have to prepare. For one thing, there's the whole magnetic factor." She tapped her lips thoughtfully.

"The—what's that?"

Sera looked at Riq. "Tell her," she said with a shrug.

"The magnetic factor," Riq said, "is"—he glanced sidelong at Sera—"a force field."

"What does it do?"

"It, ah, it pulls anything metal with you when you travel. Which can really mess things up," he said.

"It's why we don't bring coins with us," Sera continued. "We can't risk using the device at all until any coins or jewelry are stored in a separate room. Any loose metal at all."

Riq looked at a Warden's saber with disdain. "That includes weapons. But don't worry, you've still got us outnumbered."

Ilsa narrowed her eyes. "All right," she said, her voice flat. She instructed her men to put their weapons, jewelry, and coins in the room next door. A few of them hesitated, but no one dared speak out against an order. Finally, Ilsa turned back to Sera. "Show me how it works," she said more forcefully this time, holding the Infinity Ring out but gripping it tightly.

Sera didn't take it. Instead, she tilted her head and shrugged. "Okay. Where do you want to go?"

"I want to go to the future to see myself and . . . and everything I've accomplished."

"So, maybe twenty years into the future?" Sera asked with a sweet smile. "We need to be very precise."

"Y-yes. Twenty years from today." She didn't sound totally confident.

"Great. Go ahead and program the longitudinal and latitudinal coordinates, and don't forget to consider the tilt and speed of the Earth, daylight savings time, leap years, and Groundhog Day." Sera clasped her hands behind her back. "Let me know if you have questions."

Ilsa stared at the Infinity Ring. Her lips formed a thin black line. She shoved the Infinity Ring back at Sera, poking her in the stomach with it, which Sera thought was a bit on the rude side. "You do it," Ilsa demanded. "You're coming with me."

Sera perked up. "Oh! Why, thank you. I'd love to." She took the Infinity Ring and started working at it, plugging in numbers, looking off into space, adding and subtracting, tilting her head, thinking about Groundhog Day. After a few minutes of constant tapping on the instrument, she gave the Ring one last serious stare, and then she looked up. "All right," she said solemnly. "It's ready. Are you ready?"

Ilsa nodded, gripping one end of the Ring.

Sera flashed a glance at Dak and Riq, and smiled. "Okay, great. We're going to December blahblah, eighteen-abibble!" And just like that, they were gone.

A Very Short Trip

THERE WAS a moment of stunned silence. Even Dak was surprised—he hadn't expected Sera to actually warp away with Ilsa. He could only imagine what the SQ agents must be thinking as they looked on with amazement at the spot where their leader had been.

The moment passed quickly. James ran immediately to the corner and crouched into a ball, while the Hystorians sprang into action at the utterance of the secret word.

Dak and Riq joined in the fight as Hake or Stuckey (Dak couldn't remember who was who) reacted to the surprise attack by turning and punching Thomas Garrett in the mouth.

"Hey!" Dak yelled. "Don't be messing with my friend!" He screamed into the jerk's ear as Riq belted the guy in the gut.

Amidst the yelling and screaming, kicking and karate chopping, Sera and Ilsa reappeared in the exact spot they'd been standing in moments before. Ilsa looked traumatized. She screamed, pulling away from Sera and throwing herself against the nearest wall. Sera followed, neatly slapping a dangling shackle around the woman's wrist, before collapsing practically at Ilsa's feet.

"Are you okay?" Riq asked her as he followed her lead, shackling Hake to the wall with the help of Gamaliel Bailey.

"I just need a minute," she gasped.

She took less than half a minute, though, before deciding that she needed to join the fray. Slipping the Ring back into its satchel, she ran to the small closet she'd seen earlier and grabbed two spare shackle chains. She tossed one to Harriet Tubman, and together they took on several beastly Time Wardens, driving the men to the back of the room with their swinging chains. The Wardens willingly closed the shackles around their own wrists with the promise that the women would put their chains down.

"Sera!" Dak called out as he kicked a guy in the shin. "You guys look like you're acting out a scene from that online game you play, *Dungeons and More Dungeons*. Chain fights, sword fights . . . wow, just look at Ms. Tubman go!"

"Hmm," said Harriet.

On the other side of the room, an SQ agent lifted a chair to slam down on Riq's head.

"Hey!" hollered Thomas Garrett. "Don't be messing with my friend." He'd heard Dak say it moments before, and he really seemed to like the sound of it. He ran up behind the guy, grabbed the chair legs, lifted his foot, and kicked the guy square in the kidneys, sending him sprawling toward the next open spot on the wall, where Sera shackled him. The Hystorian reached out a hand to help Riq up.

"Nice one, Mr. Garrett," Riq said. "Thanks."

"You're welcome, son. Who's next?" He turned to look at the sprawled bodies of the defeated, most of whom were now chained to the walls.

Being sorely beaten, the remaining few SQ agents turned on their heels and fled. All was soon quiet.

From the corner, James peeked through his fingers. "Can I come out yet?"

Riq laughed and ran over to the boy, lifting him high in the air.

The Hystorians, nursing minor cuts and bruises, were beaming through their pain. Dak couldn't stop grinning, too. "Man," he said. "That was the best fight I've ever seen, and the war doesn't even start until –"

"Eighteen-abibble," Riq said, shushing Dak with a look.

∞

Following their victory, Dak chattered excitedly with the Hystorians, many of whom hadn't realized the kids were from the future until they'd seen what the Infinity Ring could do. Sera spoke quietly with a young woman named Susan, who wore a lovely brooch at her neck. But Riq stood aside with James and watched. He had a small smile on his face, but inside . . . inside, he was choking up a little. Maybe a lot.

He caught Harriet Tubman's eye and walked over to her. "Let's go find your niece," he said. He put a hand on Thomas Garrett's sleeve. "Can you show us where the cellar is?"

Together they walked through the hallways of Thomas Garrett's home to one of several secret rooms, then climbed down a set of stairs to the cellar. Mr. Garrett held a lantern, and Harriet called out, "Kissy? We're coming for you!"

"Aunt Minty?" cried Kissy, stepping out of the darkness, with John right behind.

"Mama!" shouted James. He leapt from Riq's arms and ran to his mother, throwing his arms around her.

"James!" Kissy sobbed, falling to her knees as her son buried his face in her dress. After a moment she looked up at Riq, tears streaming down her face. "I don't know how it could ever be possible to thank you," she said.

Riq stood in the cellar's shadows as Kissy and her aunt Minty embraced. Kissy recounted their story, telling how they were captured within sight of Federal Hill. The story made Riq shudder, knowing it could have been him. Harriet told of her capture as well. "This reunion almost didn't happen," Harriet Tubman said. She looked at Riq. "We owe a lot to you," she said. She held out her hand, drawing him into their family circle.

"And I owe my life to you," Riq said. "I feel . . . I feel as though you were family. Somehow." He couldn't look at them. Before today, they *had* been family. But now, as long as Kissy and John remained safe the rest of the way to freedom in Canada, Kessiah wouldn't end up in the South again, which is where she'd need to be in order to have the exact child that was Riq's great-great-great-grandfather. She might have more children, different children, but they couldn't be the same. Their lives would be vastly different. Their stories would be foreign to Grandma Phoebe's scrapbook.

Grandma Phoebe's scrapbook wouldn't even exist. And neither would she.

Riq's bottom lip quivered. Even surrounded by so many people, he felt more alone than ever before.

Harriet watched him solemnly, and then she embraced him. "After all you've done for us? You'll be the child I never had," she said in a gruff voice. "There. Now we're family. Got it?"

Riq laughed in spite of his sorrow. "You're totally legit," he said.

A Parting Gift

THOMAS GARRETT might not have had much furniture left, but his pantry was full enough to feed a small army of Hystorians. Dak was in his element again, surrounded by people who were living history. And shaping it.

Some of them he knew from history books. Others he didn't. Maybe since they'd exposed the SQ's plot and captured the ringleader, everyone here would now go on to be famous.

But that wasn't really the point, Dak thought. They were all fighting to change the course of history. They would accomplish far more together than any of them could hope to accomplish alone. And now Dak and his friends were a part of that, too.

So were his parents. Somehow, wherever they were, they'd known that he would need their help today. And they'd come through. Maybe everything would turn out okay, despite the odds.

He hoped the odds against the abolitionists would be a little bit easier now, at least. The SQ was still out there, but with any luck the abolitionists would take advantage of their second chance and go on to do great things.

That was the best thing about history, after all: the opportunity to learn from the mistakes of your past.

Mistakes like burning off somebody's eyebrows, for instance.

∞

Riq was able to find a quiet corner of Mr. Garrett's house, where he pulled out the SQuare. He should have been solving the puzzle to figure out where they would go next, but instead he opened the SQuare's journal, where Dak sometimes recorded the details of their adventures. He started a new file.

For a lover of languages, Riq didn't spend a lot of time writing. He didn't tend to tell stories. He didn't really feel he had interesting stories to tell.

But he had his grandma Phoebe's stories. Riq realized that if he disappeared now—if he had uprooted his entire family tree while fixing this Break—well, that was a sacrifice he was willing to make if it meant saving everyone else. He couldn't sacrifice his grandma's stories, though. He wanted them to live on.

So Riq typed late into the night. He recorded every detail of his family tree as he remembered it. Every detail about his grandma. And his parents.

He hoped that even if he didn't survive what came next, Dak and Sera would be able to keep these stories safe.

∞

Sera looked around Thomas Garrett's house. She was a little bit in awe of a man who so humbly refused to take credit for the huge sacrifice he'd made. He'd been forced to pay his last dollar in fines for helping fugitive slaves. He'd had to admit to his own friends and neighbors that yes, he had helped their slaves escape, and he'd said to them, "Just what are you going to do about it, kill me? Go ahead." Even after all that, he was more dedicated than ever to his calling and quest. His home was and would always be a safe house—as long as he was alive and had the means to help, he would help. When Sera had a moment alone with him and asked him what he most wanted, his simple reply was, "Freedom for all."

She wanted to warn him how long it would take, how many obstacles there would be. She wished she could tell him that they had magically fixed everything and tomorrow, all would be equal. But she knew that wasn't true. Things were still messed up. Real change took time.

"Communication is really important," she told him instead. "And so is keeping the SQ far away from the Underground Railroad. If you guys all stick together, and do what you did today to fight off the SQ, you might just have something big happening here."

Thomas Garrett smiled. "Thank you," he said, hand over his heart.

And then Sera drew something from her sailor pants pocket and held it up to the lantern light so he could see it. It dangled and glittered, catching the reflection of the jumping flames. She took his bruised wrist and turned it, palm up, and then she set the gold chain in his hand. "This is very, very old," she said. She showed him the tiny stamp with the year 885 engraved on it. "One of the links is broken, but it's still worth a lot." She closed his fingers over it. "You can sell this to keep things going for the abolitionsists, okay? You need it a lot more than I do."

Thomas Garrett looked at his closed fist, and then he looked at Sera. He knew better than to say no to the *Dungeons and More Dungeons* master, and so he simply smiled and said, "Thank you."

Safe Passages

GAMALIEL BAILEY and most of the other abolitionists were eager to get home after their long absences. There was room enough for those who stayed behind to sleep in Thomas Garrett's house. Sera finally got the bath she so desperately wanted, and Dak and Riq each bathed, too, at Sera's insistence. Donning her dry Quaker garb once again, she joined the others at dawn to take the chained SQ to jail for endangering and threatening the lives of children and adults alike. Not even the Fugitive Slave Act could protect them after all they'd done.

Riq couldn't help but notice that Ilsa was taking their defeat especially hard. He'd expected her to resist or make threats, but she remained quiet. Almost eerily so.

After they'd gotten rid of Ilsa and the rest, they all headed to the train station, where Harriet Tubman and John Bowley, who had their free papers, accompanied a very large, very fragile crate on a one-way trip to Ontario, Canada. Harriet would be back, she promised. But first she'd see to it that Kissy and her family made it safely all the way. "It's the most amazing feeling," Harriet said, "standing in freedom. Seeing your free fingers, your free toes, your free everything." She embraced Riq. "Will we ever see you again?"

"I don't think so," Riq said.

"Well, if you're ever in New York, come by," she said with a shy grin, handing him a piece of paper. "That's where I'm going to build my dream home once this is all over."

Riq took the paper and hugged the tiny woman. "Thank you," he said.

Dak, Sera, and Riq walked back to Thomas Garrett's house with the man himself and with the real Mrs. Beeson, who would be making the trip back to Cambridge on the same pilot cutter on which Sera and Dak had been passengers. "Tell them all thank you for me," Sera said. "And please give Captain Grunder his pants back."

Dak snorted. He poked Riq. "Captain Grunder pants. Get it?"

"No."

"That book about—"

"No."

"The two guys and their—"

"NO."

"All right, all right already. You guys are so serious all the time."

Riq ignored Dak and turned to Mrs. Beeson. "There's something that's been bothering me since we first arrived," he said. "There's a shed near your house. Does it have a trap door in it?"

"Thee are a smart lad, I see," Mrs. Beeson said. "Indeed it does. It is one of my hiding places on the farm."

"We saw the floor move," he said. "I wondered if someone has been hiding there."

"I believe it. Before I was overtaken, I told a fugitive to take a lantern and go there. I'd suspected something, told him it wasn't safe in the house. I'm glad he made it. I'll check it upon my return. Thank thee for the information."

"Leave it to us to run away from an actual safe house and into a trap," Dak said.

"Oh," Sera said. "That reminds me—I apologize for any sticky soda mess you might find in the cellar. It was our only way to escape."

"Have no worries," Mrs. Beeson said with a puzzled smile, surely having no idea what the girl was talking about. "Your escape was of most importance. I am blessed to have had you in my home, and sorry for the circumstances encompassing it."

Sera held up a hand. "High five?"

Mrs. Beeson made a fist instead and held it out for the bump. "Thee are legit," she said.

38

A Glimpse Forward

THE THREE time travelers decided to catch up with one another before going directly to their next mission. They sat in a meadow nearby, the weak December sun warming their shoulders.

"This was a tough Break in a different way than we're used to," Sera mused. She looked at Riq. "For you especially, I mean. Do you wish we hadn't come here?"

Riq wrapped his fingers around a piece of long yellow grass and pulled. He chewed on one end of it. "At first I hated this place. This time period. I still do, but you know what? It was really heartening to see all the abolitionists just being so . . . so committed like that, you know?" He paused. "Not just committed to being Hystorians, I mean, but to being, well, so human. It puts . . . it helps put things into perspective."

Dak nodded. "It makes me want to be like them with the work that we're doing."

"Me, too," Sera said. "I wish we could know what kind

of difference they'll make now."

"Didn't you already have a glimpse of the future with old stony-faced Ilsa?" Dak asked.

"Yeah, where did you go, anyway?" Riq asked.

Sera's face paled. She looked at the ground. "Nowhere, actually. I, um, I programmed the Infinity Ring to five seconds in the future, so we'd blip out and back in again. I just wanted to cause a distraction for you guys."

Dak grinned. "Well, in that case, since you didn't waste a trip earlier, maybe we can do it now?"

Sera bit her lip. "I don't know, Dak. The Infinity Ring isn't a toy."

"I think we should," Riq blurted. "Just this once, I'd like to know how things turned out." He took a deep breath and blew it out. "If nothing else, I need to know what happened to James."

Dak turned to Sera. "You can't say no to that!"

Sera shrugged. "Okay. Let's go forward a bit and see."

"Yes!" said Dak.

"Listen, Dak," Riq said. "I already told Sera, but I'm saying this to you, too. If anything, like, *happens* to me when we leave here, just . . . keep going."

Dak frowned. "You sound like a funeral. What's up?"

"Is it your Remnants?" Sera asked.

Riq nodded. "Yeah. But I think they'll be over as soon as Kissy makes it to Canada. They just leave me feeling a little strange, I guess. Ignore me."

"I always do," Dak said, and punched Riq in the arm.

Riq turned his head slowly and raised an eyebrow.

"I've got thirty pounds on you, little bro, and I will kick your butt if I have to. Don't push it."

With a sigh, Sera flopped back in the grass and pulled out the Infinity Ring just as Thomas Garrett walked up.

"I wanted to say good-bye. It was a delight to know you," he said. "May I ask where you'll go next? Or is that a secret?"

"Nah, we can tell you," Dak said. "We're going a few years into the future to see how things turned out."

"Any specifics, Mr. Smyth? Mr. Jones?" Sera asked them, poised to enter coordinates into the Ring.

Riq perked up. "As a matter of fact," he said, "I do have a place in mind." He pulled the paper from his pocket and handed it to Sera. "Harriet Tubman's house in Auburn, New York."

Dak nodded. "That sounds awesome. Make it, like, 1875ish? The *ahem ahem* war-abibble *should* be over by then, if you get what I'm saying." He waggled his eyebrows. "Pick a day, any day."

Riq looked up. "How about July 4?"

Dak grinned. "That's absolutely perfect."

Sera started her calculations. "Okay," she said when she was finished. They called out a round of good-byes to Thomas Garrett, and within seconds, they were catapulting through time and space. When they opened their eyes, they were standing in a very hot kitchen where a short woman stood on a small stool in front of a stove, stirring stew in a large pot as if she were expecting guests.

Conductor, Healer, Soldier, Spy

RIQ'S FIRST thought was *I'm still here.*

He hadn't been totally sure he would survive the warp. Sera had said once that as long as they were traveling through time, the three of them were anomalies. Being anomalies meant that changes in the time stream wouldn't affect them, no matter how much history changed around them.

It was good to know she'd been right about that.

Then he realized they were standing smack-dab in the middle of Harriet Tubman's kitchen. He flashed Sera a look, knowing their sudden appearance could scare the poor woman. "You couldn't land us on the front step?" he muttered.

She glared and shoved the Infinity Ring at him. "You want to do this? Say the word, smarty-pants."

Riq sighed. "Good point. Sorry." He rapped on the wall lightly and cleared his throat.

Harriet Tubman, now in her mid-fifties, turned at the

noise. She set down her wooden spoon with a *bang* and a hand went to her lips. "Oh, my stars," she said, her voice as rough as a sailor's. "My adopted son has come home." She stepped down from her stool and walked to the time travelers, reaching out to take Riq's hands in her own. "Come in and sit. We've been expecting you."

"We?" asked Dak. He sounded as if he were afraid they'd stepped into another trap.

But the young man who came around the corner had a huge smile on his face. "Riq!" he exclaimed in a booming voice.

Riq hesitated a moment.

"It's James!" hissed Sera, poking Riq with her elbow.

Riq's face broke into a wide smile. "Hey! I didn't expect to see you!"

James gave each of the time travelers a hug as Harriet Tubman watched.

"Do you have a few minutes?" she asked.

Riq smiled again. "I think we can spare a few."

"So," Dak began. "We last saw you in eighteen-fifty."

"Or as I like to remember it, eighteen-abibble," Harriet said. She smiled.

Dak grinned back. "Nicely played. Hey, does that mean my little phrase caught on? Is everybody saying it now?"

Harriet shook her head. "No. No one is."

"Oh." Dak glanced at Sera, who just shook her head

and laughed. "Okay, so what happened after we saw you?"

"Well, Mr. Thomas Garrett immediately let me know I might expect to see you today," Harriet said, eyes merry. "So I made a note to remind myself and kept it in my hat all these years. And I just knew James would want to see you, too, so I let him know and he came down from Canada."

"That's right," James said with a smile.

Harriet recounted her trip aboard the train to freedom, with Kissy, James, and the baby inside the crate, and Harriet, John, and the other Hystorians causing distractions whenever the baby cried or James couldn't contain his own frustration at being in one more confined space. "James was a pistol on that trip, the poor boy, but he's grateful to have taken it," she said. "He remembers it well; don't you, dear?"

"Like it happened yesterday," James said. "But what I really remember is being sad that you weren't there in Canada. Nobody was able to play the horseback game as well as you—they all tired out too fast," he said with a laugh. "I talked about you to anyone who would listen. I called you my best friend. I'm pretty sure the other kids thought you were imaginary, but Mom always told me I'd see you again."

Riq didn't know what to say. He laughed hard so he could pretend like his misty eyes were from laughter. "I remember it like it was yesterday, too," he said, rubbing his back. "In fact, it *was* yesterday. I'm still sore."

Sera narrowed her eyes at Riq. She tapped her fingers on her knee as he wiped his eyes. He had a feeling she suspected something. She flashed him a sympathetic smile, and said to Harriet, "Tell us about the Underground Railroad. Did it continue?"

Harriet nodded her head, almost in wonder. "Yes, the Underground Railroad continued, to the utter consternation of the SQ. The harder they worked to stop us, the harder we fought to keep it going. And it grew. Slaves escaped, told their stories, and word got out about the true situation in the South. I went back and forth to personally guide as many slaves as I could to freedom. And of course, my friend Harriet Beecher Stowe's book really started jaws a-wagging."

"*Uncle Tom's Cabin*?" Dak guessed.

"That's right. And your friend Gamaliel, God rest his soul, was the first to publish it."

The three time travelers gasped in unison. "Rest his soul?" Sera said quietly.

Harriet nodded sadly. "He never lived to see emancipation. But he fought for it until his last breath." She added, "Thomas Garrett is gone, too. He'd become such a dear friend—helping hundreds more slaves after you left. It seems he'd received a very, *very* generous"—she glanced sidelong at Sera—"anonymous donation. It kept him in business for years to come."

Sera bit her lip in silent glee. Riq knew she must have had something to do with that. But she only said, "Oh? How nice."

"Any chance there was a president named Lincoln?" Dak asked.

"Yes, indeed. He was decent, though I had to give him a piece of my mind a time or two about allowing slavery to continue in the South." She frowned. "Took us a few years of war to convince him."

"So there was a civil war?" Dak asked. "When did it start?"

"Oh yes, there was a civil war. Eighteen sixty-one to eighteen sixty-five. It was tough and it was messy, but the abolitionists won in the end."

"Only four years?" Dak said. "That's better than fifteen, but . . ."

"I know," said Sera. "I was hoping it wouldn't happen at all."

James nodded. "Everything was demolished—all through that land we traveled from Cambridge on north, and all over the country. Aunt Minty was in the middle of it all. As a conductor for the Underground Railroad for eight years, she made over a dozen trips into slave territory to rescue fugitives. She was a nurse for the injured, a recruiter of over five hundred slaves to be soldiers for the North, and even a Union spy."

Harriet only smiled.

"Wow, a spy?" Riq said with a grin. "My grandma Phoebe would be —" He stopped abruptly and took in a sharp breath. Then he stood up and walked to the window. "Never mind. I'm sorry."

Harriet and James shared a quiet look, and then James

got up and followed Riq to the window while Harriet ushered Dak and Sera to the kitchen for some stew.

At the window, James put his hand on Riq's shoulder. "We really are related, aren't we?"

Riq leaned forward, gripping his head in his hands. He swallowed hard. And then he shook his head. "I don't know," he whispered. "I don't know anything anymore."

They stood in silence for a long moment. "Thank you for saving my life," James whispered. "I grew up free and happy because of you. No matter what, you will always be my brother."

All Riq could do was nod. "Thanks," he choked out. "That means more than you know."

After a moment, Riq wiped his face with his hands, took a deep breath, and smiled. He and James walked into the kitchen and sat with Sera and Dak in front of steaming bowls of stew. He could feel Sera's eyes on him.

"Whatever happened to Ilsa?" Dak asked.

Harriet frowned. "She disappeared after you did," she said. "People said she'd gone insane. But every now and then I get a strange feeling coming over me, like she's got me in her crosshairs. Like if I turned my head an inch more, I'd see her wild red hair disappearing around a corner." Harriet tapped her lips thoughtfully. "The woman clearly made an impression on me. But that's all in my imagination, I'm sure."

"The SQ has eyes and ears everywhere," Sera said, remembering what Brint and Mari had told them. "You've done so much to weaken them—I'm sure they're tracking you, and I'm sure they're really mad. Be careful, Ms. Tubman."

Harriet only laughed. "The SQ ain't never caught me yet."

When Riq and the others rose to leave, James and Harriet embraced them all one by one. "You were an inspiration to us all in a dark, dark time—not just for African-American rights, but for women's rights, too. Whatever you said to my friend Susan B. Anthony really got her going. Thank you for your service to the Hystorians," Harriet said, "and for your great sacrifices." She gave Riq a look that could only come from a battered hero like Harriet. "Whatever they may be."

∞

Sera led Dak and Riq out of Harriet Tubman's home the traditional way, through the front door, to catch one more glimpse of the nineteenth century while Riq used the SQuare, working out the puzzle for the next Break.

"You know what would be fun?" Sera said as they strolled along. "Going to some tropical island with lots of food and soap and toothbrushes, where the Break could only be fixed by us taking a vacation."

"Boring," Dak said. "I want to go back to Paris."

"What? Not the Vikings again!"

"No, not 885. Late 1700s kind of Paris."

Riq tuned in as he worked the SQuare. "Why there?"

Sera laughed. "I know why," she said. "He wants to get another bottle of soda."

"So what? I'm a collector!"

Riq shook his head and turned back to the SQuare. "Well," he said, "you may get your island getaway, Sera."

Sera gasped. "Really? Are you serious? Where! Tahiti? Barbados? Canary Islands? New Zealand? Tell me!" She gripped his arm. "Come on!"

Riq flashed a grin. "*Hmm,* so very close. How about this—ready? Are you sitting down?"

Sera shook his arm. "Of course not. We're walking, dog breath."

"Well?" Dak asked, impatient.

"Okay," Riq said. "Picture this: gorgeous sunrise over the water on a steamy—"

"Just tell me!" Sera said. "*Ooh,* I can feel the sand between my toes now."

"That's probably just silt in your socks from the Chesapeake Bay," Dak remarked.

Riq's eyes danced for the first time in days. "Okay, okay. We're going to Japan. Not exactly tropical, but it's an island. And there will be samurai. And maybe ninjas. The clue's a little unclear on that point."

Sera's jaw dropped. Dak's did, too. And then he grinned and pumped the air with his fist. "Yes!"

"Oy," Sera said, shaking her head. "I hate my life right now. I really do. That was pretty stinking mean, Riq."

"You're just so fun to tease," Riq said.

They rounded the corner where a stately farmhouse stood, a large cornfield behind it. This time the stalks were vibrant green and only knee high. Sera reluctantly pulled out the Infinity Ring and began to program the year and the location coordinates.

"Don't forget to factor in Groundhog Day," Dak deadpanned.

Groundhog Day. The term made Sera's stomach clench when she realized what Dak was referring to—her time warp with Ilsa.

Sera hadn't told them the truth about that.

And the truth was: She'd made a horrible mistake with her calculations.

She'd seen the Cataclysm with her own eyes.

Get a grip, Froste! she told herself, determined not to let the stress show. She couldn't bring herself to tell Dak or Riq what she had witnessed. She would just have to be strong enough to carry that particular burden alone.

As she finished the last few calculations, the door of the farmhouse burst open and a towering, chiseled-faced woman with white hair—and red undertones—came charging out at them.

The three time travelers looked at one another wearily.

"*Annnd* our lives would just not be complete without a visit from Ilsa," Sera muttered.

"Man, Mr. Garrett could *not* keep a secret," Dak said.

"She does look a little crazy," Riq added.

I think I know why, Sera thought. But she kept it to herself. "Grab hold, boys. We're five, four, three, two, one, and—"

Gone.

PLAY THE GAME

Infinity Ring • Episode 3
THE WAY OF THE WARRIOR

Japan's greatest samurai is on a quest . . . and he needs *your* help to complete it.

Explore a Japanese castle!

Solve the Art of Memory puzzle!

The adventure unfolds in the Infinity Ring game. Log on now to live history.

Fix the past. Save the future.

infinityring.com

READ THE BOOK

Infinity Ring • Book 4

CURSE OF THE ANCIENTS

Dak, Sera, and Riq are stranded in the time of the Ancient Mayans! What mystery will they uncover — and how will it change their mission forever?

The book comes with an all-new, top secret Hystorian's Guide – which unlocks the next episode of the Infinity Ring game.

Fix the past. Save the future.

infinityring.com